T0286049

STAR TREK™
EXPLORER

THE OFFICIAL MAGAZINE

PRESENTS

"THE MISSION" AND OTHER STORIES

STAR TREK EXPLORER

THE OFFICIAL MAGAZINE

PRESENTS

"THE MISSION" AND OTHER STORIES

The short stories contained in the book feature characters and situations from across the *Star Trek* universe, including *Star Trek: Enterprise, Star Trek, Star Trek: The Next Generation, Star Trek: Deep Space Nine,* and *Star Trek: Voyager.*

These mini-epics include the return of noir detective Dixon Hill, a strange tale of the crew of the *Enterprise*-D forgetting their first officer, William Riker, a dramatic prelude to the classic episode "What Are Little Girls Made Of?" and even a story showcasing Captain Jonathan Archer's loyal hound, Porthos.

EDITORIAL
Editor: Jonathan Wilkins
Designer: Dan Bura
Group Editor: Jake Devine
Assistant Editors: Phoebe Hedges & Calum Collins
Editorial Assistant: Ibraheem Kazi
Art Director: Oz Browne
Production Controllers: Caterina Falqui & Kelly Fenlon
Production Manager: Jackie Flook
Marketing Coordinator: Lauren Noding
Publicist: Caitlin Storer
Publicity & Sales Coordinator: Alexandra Iciek
Sales & Circulation Manager: Steve Tothill

Digital & Marketing Manager: Jo Teather
Head of Creative & Business Development: Duncan Baizley
Publishing Directors: Ricky Claydon & John Dziewiatkowski
Group Operations Director: Alex Ruthen
Executive Vice President: Andrew Sumner
Publishers: Vivian Cheung & Nick Landau

DISTRIBUTION
U.S. Distribution: Penguin Random House
U.K. Distribution: MacMillan Distribution
Direct Sales Market: Diamond Comic Distributors
General Inquiries: customerservice@titanpublishingusa.com

Star Trek Explorer Presents "The Mission" and Other Stories
ISBN: 9781787739635
Published by Titan Magazines
A division of Titan Publishing Group Ltd., 144 Southwark Street, London SE1 0UP, TM ® & © 2023 CBS Studios Inc. © 2023 Paramount Pictures. STAR TREK and Related Marks are Trademarks of CBS Studios Inc. All Rights Reserved. Titan Authorised User. CBS, the CBS Eye logo and related marks are trademarks of CBS Broadcasting Inc. TM & © 2023 CBS Broadcasting Inc. All rights reserved.

A CIP catalogue record for this title is available from the British Library.
First Edition December 2023
10 9 8 7 6 5 4 3 2 1
Printed in China.

Paramount Global: Marian Cordry
Copyright Promotions Ltd.: Anna Hatjoullis
Paramount Home Entertainment: Kate Addy, Jiella Esmat, Liz Hadley, and John Robson
Simon & Schuster US: Ed Schlesinger

Contents

Control

STORY: JOHN PEEL
ILLUSTRATION: LOUIE DE MARTINIS

Chark was hunting. Normally, this was simply a matter of it sliding through the scrubby brush until it drew close enough to a victim to be able to feel its thoughts. Chark could then send out its thought controls that would compel its victim to see the hunter as something harmless and comforting until Chark was close enough to pounce and extrude its feeding tubules and absorb the life-energy of its victim – along with the memories and thoughts of its prey. Chark learned from these memories, making it a swifter and more deadly predator. Generally it could find a Swift Four-Leg or even a Slouching Two-Leg without difficulty, but for some reason its hunting was resulting in nothing at all this day. Chark cast out its mental web as far as it would reach, but neither Four-Legs or Two-Legs were within range.

This was not a real problem quite yet. Chark was only mildly hungry. But Chark was small, and rather shapeless, and could only travel quite slowly. It might be hours before something came within its mental range, and *that* could be troublesome. Why were there no potential prey beasts within range? This had never happened in all of Chark's experience. There were *always* potential victims, and yet... now, there were none. It was disturbing.

And then there was *something*, at the edge of Chark's senses; something the hunter had never felt before. It wasn't a prey animal Chark had ever come across before. It had a very strange feel to it. But it was coming closer, and soon Chark would be able to read its thoughts. But this strange creature was obviously the cause of the missing prey animals. It felt *wrong* somehow, though not exactly dangerous. But it must have troubled the Four-Legs and Two-Legs and caused them to flee. Well, it may have caused the problem for Chark, but it was able to think, and so it could be the solution to Chark's troubles. As soon as it came close enough, Chark would attack this *stranger* and so feast. End of problem.

As it drew closer, Chark could read its thoughts and emotions more clearly. And became more and more disturbed. This was not a prey beast of any kind. And its thoughts were stranger and more complex than any Chark had ever absorbed before. Unlike any animal Chark has ever encountered, this creature had an odd awareness. It had purpose and determination, and not to do with eating. It was... *curious*. It was looking for things, and it didn't even know what things it was seeking. Anything that caught its attention, that appeared interesting.

It made no sense.

And... it was really intelligent. Intelligent in a way Chark had never experienced before. Its thoughts darted in complex fashions, centering on many things at once. Most animals thought of food or a safe place to rest, but those ideas were very low in this one's consciousness. It was focused mostly on looking for... rocks. Rocks? That made no sense to Chark, and he pulled further at the threads of thought. And it was loss for a few seconds in a web of complicated thoughts.

The beast gave itself a *name*. A designation to identify itself to others. How bizarre! *Lieutenant Savannah Preston...* Or *Vanna* to her closest friends. And with that thought came a very disturbing image of this Vanna doing complex and disgusting things with another member of her species...

Her... This creature had two sexes! Frankly, Chark could not comprehend this. It was something to do with making offspring, though what this Vanna beast had been doing wasn't with the aim of reproduction but entertainment. It made absolutely no sense – any reasonable creature would reproduce as Chark did – by feasting and then splitting into two equal halves. This was some vague information in her mind that any offspring she produced would be small and helpless and in dire need of looking after, lest it become prey. *Absurd!*

Well, it wasn't interesting or relevant, even if it was close to the surface of Vanna's mind and thus presumably important to her. Chark scurried about in this strange mind some more, and discovered even weirder things. This Vanna thing wasn't native to Chark's world!

Wait, what was a *world*? Chark followed the thread, and was almost paralyzed by what it revealed. This place where Chark lived was a world, it seemed. It wasn't flat and endless, as Chark had always assumed, but a roundish thing that hovered in... well, nothing. Again, it was meaningless at the moment to Chark. But it seemed that there were lots and lots of these floating balls spread out in nothingness. And this Vanna was of some kind of a construction that could move through the nothing from world to world. She called it the *U.S.S. Enterprise*, and she was attached to it by fondness and duty. And she had what she called a *job* on this *Enterprise* as a geologist. She studied rocks, and they somehow told her things. Well, this explained her odd interest in rocks, at least, even if it made no logical sense.

WHY WERE THERE NO POTENTIAL PREY BEASTS
WITHIN RANGE? THIS HAD NEVER HAPPENED IN ALL
OF CHARK'S EXPERIENCE...

All of this time, the Vanna creature was drawing closer, and her thoughts were growing clearer and more complex, and making more sense. In just a few moments, Chark could leap out at her and start to feast. While it waited, though, Chark probed deeper into the mind of this new thing that had arrived. The *Enterprise*, it seemed, was moving from world to world on some sort of quest that Chark couldn't make any sense of. But there was life on many of these worlds. And Vanna had never heard of any creature like Chark on any such world.

There were no predators like Chark on these other worlds. And there were hundreds – if not thousands or more – of potential prey.

And the *Enterprise* traveled freely from one world to another…

If Chark went along with this *Enterprise*, then it would never have

problems feeding again. There would be prey everywhere, prey that didn't know about Chark and had no protection against Chark's mind power.

And a new thought, something that had never before occurred to Chark, seized the killer: there was no need to kill this Vanna thing. Chark could make her see it as something desirable, like one of the silly rocks she sought, and she would take it back to the *Enterprise* with her.

And there would be lots and lots of food there.

The more Chark considered this new concept, the more it liked it. With its ability to control what these *Enterprise* creatures saw, Chark could keep a reserve of future victims that would never, ever see Chark as a predator. Chark could feast as much as it liked, and gain strength to split into two beings. And each new world that the *Enterprise* flew to, one or

more Charks could remain behind and feast forever…

The future was unlimited. To eat and breed and spread unrestricted, and the Vanna creature and her kind would unwittingly aid Chark's plans. This was a destiny Chark had never seen before, but it could not pass up this huge potential. And the first step was to control the Vanna.

She was close enough now for Chark to perceive her directly, instead of just through her thoughts. She was a Two-Leg, but not like any Chark had feasted on it the past. She had a very strange appearance, all bumps and curves and other odd shapes that meant nothing to Chark but that obviously appealed to others of her herd. Chark focused on appearing innocent and alluring to her, and he could feel the wave of pleasure passing through her as she "saw" how Chark imitated a small

rock specimen. Happily, the Vanna snatched up the predator and stored it in a pouch.

Chark's plan was working. It remained in its impersonation of a pretty rock while she did various other odd and uninteresting things, and then it felt her intent to return to this *Enterprise*. She talked to a small thing, telling it: "Preston to *Enterprise*. One to beam up."

For a moment, Chark was gripped by sheer terror. A strange, horrifying sensation crept across its body. Chark wanted to lash out somehow, but couldn't feel anything there to react against. And then, confusingly, it found itself in a strange enclosure. It was made mostly of metal, but it was somehow pervaded by light. Chark could sense another Vanna close by the first, one that had not been close a second before, and then, as its emotions slowed down and it could react normally again, it felt many, many more of the Vanna creatures.

"Welcome back, Lieutenant," the new Vanna said.

"Thanks," the old one replied, holding up the sample bag with Chark inside. "Lots of great samples this time."

"Have fun playing with your rocks," the second Vanna said. The first one laughed and walked to one of the metal walls. Part of it opened up and allowed her through into a longer, thinner metal room. Chark could feel dozens of other Vanna creatures all around. She had returned to her herd.

Now it was time to plan. Chark knew that no matter how large a herd was, it always had a single leader – the one who made the decisions, and led the others. The strongest, wisest, wiliest member of the herd – that was one Chark needed. If it could control the mind of that one, then it could control the herd. Chark burrowed into the thoughts of the Vanna carrying it, and there was the answer. The leader was an Archer.

That was who Chark needed. But where in this *Enterprise* of enclosed metal rooms was the Archer to be found? Chark nudged the thoughts of the Vanna, who promptly crossed to what she thought of as a *computer interface*, and there she typed in a query. "Captain Archer's sleeping in his room," the Vanna muttered to herself. And then: "So why do I care?" She didn't, of course, but it was vital information for Chark.

Another gentle mental push, and the Vanna went over to the Archer's resting room. It couldn't have been more perfect for Chark's plans; if the Archer slept, it would be the simplest possible procedure for the hunter to slip into this creature's mind and take it over.

Then Chark hit its first snag. He tried to get the Vanna to open the Archer's door, but she couldn't do it. Chark didn't understand it fully, but it seemed that there was a way for someone to prevent those door-things from opening if the someone wanted

IT WAS REALLY INTELLIGENT. INTELLIGENT IN A WAY CHARK HAD NEVER EXPERIENCED BEFORE…

to be alone. *That* he could understand – it was much safer to sleep alone and in somewhere protected. But the Vanna couldn't get inside the room to the Archer without waking him up.

But that didn't mean that Chark couldn't. Chark was smaller, and more flexible, and needed only a small space in which to slip. There was something called an *air conditioner* that would grant it access to the Archer's sleeping quarters. Chark concentrated its thoughts and diverted any of the local creatures from coming close, and instructed the Vanna to open the access vent. As soon as she did it, Chark erased her memories of this and of ever having seen it or the pretty stone Chark had pretended to be and dismissed the Vanna. She wondered for a moment

what she was doing outside the Captain's room, then shrugged and wandered back to her lab.

Chark oozed through the small vent and into the metal room beyond. There, on a raised portion of the floor, was the Archer, and Chark could feel the waves of sleep imprisoning the herd leader. Spreading his aura of gentleness about itself, Chark slid across the floor toward its unsuspecting victim.

There was a second being in the room, but it was neither a Vanna beast nor an Archer creature. It had a more primitive mind, not as complex as the others. It was probably some prey beast that Archer would devour upon waking. As precaution, Chark was sending out its mental waves to make the beast

see Chark as something pleasant and comforting, but the predator was not expecting any problems as it concentrated on its attack of the sleeping Archer creature.

As a result, its dying thought was: *Why didn't this ravening monster see Chark as something pleasant and appealing? How could such a simple creature see through Chark's illusions?*

Porthos gazed up at Archer, sleeping on his bed. Porthos was very attached to his human, but there were times when… well, frankly, he left something to be desired. Archer was terribly affectionate and considerate, and often gave Porthos nice surprises.

This was not one of them. Regretfully, Porthos surveyed the mess. *Worst chew toy ever.* ⌁

The Guardian

STORY: GARY RUSSELL
ILLUSTRATION: LOUIE DE MARTINIS

"We made this happen. We are responsible for everything! And now we're paying the price..."

Hob looked around, trying to locate the source of the shouting.

"Stupid fool," muttered Takhen. "He'll bring the Androids down on us in seconds."

Hob nodded. Whoever it was, they needed shutting up, and quickly. For all their sakes.

And in his peripheral vision, he saw a flicker of movement. High above them.

He poked his head round the edge of the doorway, to get a proper view. The yeller was a man in a grey suit, standing atop a burning tower block about thirty meters to their left. Hob couldn't identify him – it was a sad inditement of their situation that frankly anyone still alive in the city should be known to him as there were so few of them left. But the black smoke was obscuring his face.

Hob closed his eyes for a second.

"History will judge us harshly," the man called out. Hob knew he wasn't addressing them directly, he was just screaming out in a sort of primal fear. The sort of rage and frustration the people tended to keep bottled up. But now, as the city died around him, he'd clearly decided he no longer needed to hold it in.

"I think it's Jorel," Hob muttered to Takhen.

"Figures," she grunted back. "Never could use the brains he was born with." She grabbed Hobs arm. "We should go."

"We can't leave him. It's Jorel!"

"Yes we can," Takhen hissed "If he's lost his mind, then he's no use to anyone." She looked Hob straight in the eye. "And while he's screaming his head off, he's a good …"

She turned away, not wanting to finish the thought.

Hob finished it for her, angrily. "Distraction?

Target?" He yanked his arm out of her grip. "Is that what we've sunk to? Sacrificing our friends to save our own skins?"

After a beat, Takhen shrugged. "Yes. I want to live. If Jorel doesn't, that's his decision."

Hob suddenly placed his hand on her mouth and eased them forcefully back into the shadows, dropping closer to the floor, pulling Takhen with him.

She understood why.

Striding through the flames on the streets, the smoke, the carnage, were a group of Androids. Five of them. The orange flames reflected off their hairless skulls, their hairless arms and torsos, their entire bodies, making them seem to glow with an inner light; each one androgenous, naked and with the strength and stamina of four or five people like Hob

The Androids were, of course, untouched by the fire. Unhurt by the leaking gases and choking plasma. They walked through it all as they would a forest or a meadow.

In the days when there were forests and meadows on Exo III. Before it all went wrong and civilisation fell.

The Androids were looking up and down, left and right, their nostrils visibly enlarging as they sniffed. Every enhanced sense operating as they sought their prey.

Prey like Hob and Takhen. Prey like Jorel.

They located Jorel when he started yelling again.

"You'd think we'd have known better, but no. We had to prove to ourselves that we were superior to even nature and –"

Jorel stooped suddenly as a charred metal girder penetrated his torso. Hob winced, guessing Jorel was already dead before his legs gave way and he dropped to the burning ground below.

The Android which had thrown the girder was joined by the others, inhumane rictus grins on their faces.

Part of another building finally gave way, and in a flurry of masonry and burning timbers, it collapsed beside them, one of the Its actually getting buried by some of the molten rubble. A second later, the Android emerged, untouched, unhurt and uninterested in what had happened. They had but one purpose – extermination of everything alive on Exo III, anything that weren't Androids.

Takhen shook her head sadly. "We need to regroup, find other survivors from other cities and countries. Fight back."

Hob laughed, mirthlessly. "I'm beginning to think you and I may well be it. Lowter and the Rori brothers were supposed to meet us an hour ago."

"You think they aren't coming?"

Hob shrugged. "I think they are dead. Like Jorel. The Androids aren't leaving anything alive.

He grabbed Takhens hand. "Let's go. If we're going to die, I'd rather do it trying to escape. Trying to survive, rather than waiting here for inevitable discovery."

Takhen swallowed hard, then nodded. "We should head out into the wastelands, beyond the city rims. The caves, other survivors will have gone there."

"To where it all began? Why?"

Takhen started to move. "Because the Androids won't expect to us to go there. It's not… logical, or sensible. People like Lowter know how they think… she worked with them long enough. She said to me once it was an obvious place for people to hide.'

Hob wanted to argue, but knew he couldn't – he simply had no other suggestions. Instead, he nodded and together they moved slowly and silently through the wreckage of their once beautiful city.

Hours later, Hob and Takhen finally allowed themselves to rest, in a small copse of trees on the edge of the wastelands.

They looked back at the night sky above the city which was just one huge blur of orange, red and yellow as the whole place burned down.

Hob realised Takhen was crying, quietly. She'd been holding it in check for hours, knowing that something as natural as sobbing would be heard by the Androids astonishing hearing.

He touched her shoulder, but she shrugged it off. 'I'm okay, she said. "I'm just…"

"Sad?"

"Angry. Bitter." She rounded on him, as if it was all Hob's fault. "Look at us, look at our civilisation. Because of the Androids, we have no future. You and the other Exo Municipals decreed this, you gave them the power."

Hob shook his head. "That's not true, it was just an experiment…"

"Look at us Hob. Even if we survive the night, what's the point?

"WE NEED TO REGROUP, FIND OTHER SURVIVORS FROM OTHER CITIES AND COUNTRIES. FIGHT BACK."

We thought we could overcome the sterility, find a new way to prolong existence, keep our planet alive, even without children, but now...? Maybe Jorel was right. We did this to ourselves." And with a venom Hob hadn't anticipated, she slapped him around the face. "*You* did this. Our precious leaders. And where are we now? Our entire civilisation erased by your hubris."

"That's not fair…" Hob started to say, but the look Takhen gave him made him realise it was safer to let her vent all that anger and fury.

"Create new bodies for ourselves, you lot all said. Give ourselves immortality. Think of it, we can have time to let the fields regrow, let the rivers refill. No need to exhaust our resources. Become Androids for a few centuries. Let the planet heal and make it a place to welcome the future later. But first, give them autonomy, because we need them to help us take those first few stumbling steps...

never foreseeing they would turn on us, like ungrateful children we could never have."

Takhen wasn't even addressing Hob now, he could see that. She was just saying aloud what she had wanted to say years ago, when he'd come home, explaining the Municipals' decisions. And Takhen, who Hob knew had always wanted children with him, had accepted the decisions for the sake of society.

Now she was saying what hundreds, possible thousands of their now dead friends and colleagues, strangers and unknowns had all been thinking for years.

And maybe she was right. But that didn't change what had happened.

"Come on then," Takhen suddenly said.

"What?"

"Let's find the caves, find the catacombs where it all began. See if Lowter was right."

And she was moving again,

further out of the copse, and off across the rough wastelands.

Taking a deep breath, and giving a final look at the burning city he knew he'd never come back to, Hob followed his wife into the darkness.

It took two days to reach the cave mouth where it had started, many years ago. Hob and Takhen had rationed the fruits and water they found along the way, knowing food and drink would get more limited, the nearer they got to the catacombs.

Was Takhen ready to drop, he wondered? Hob certainly was, but he knew he needed to appear strong for his wife. He smiled inwardly. Why? Takhen was three times stronger than he was. She was certainly not going to drop. She was Takhen and at that moment, he remembered why he loved her so.

"We have arrived," she announced quietly.

Hob nodded.

Gingerly, they looked inside the

cave. It sloped down into wide cavern, high and dimly lit by some flambeaux shoved into the ground. They had burned a long way down, suggesting many days since they were lit.

Sprawled on the ground were twenty or thirty dead bodies.

And sat in the midst, cross-legged was a woman, a plastic cup in her hand.

"Lowter," Takhen breathed and crossed straight to her, picking her way through the dead, managing not to look at them.

In case they were other people she or Hob knew.

Hob followed a few paces behind.

Takhen knelt down to Lowter, shaking her shoulders.

Hob could see foam bubbled and dried around her lips. He finally glanced at the bodies, all of them with the same dried foam. Some had closed their eyes, others were staring upward in death. None of them had died easily.

"Lowter," hissed Takhen, but

Hob eased his wife away. "She's dead, too." Hob pointed at the half-full cup in Lowter's hands. "Poison. They all took it."

"But why?"

"Because they knew it was better than the Androids finding them."

Hob stared further in the darkness, down into the deep catacombs where it had all started years before. "I'm going to see what's still down there," he said. "Come on."

But Takhen said no. She was staying here. "With our friends. Our life."

Hob nodded and started to walk, a tear welling up in his eye.

He heard Takhen cough, she tried to keep it in but unsuccessfully. Then Hob heard the cup hit the stony ground. He didn't look back. He wanted to remember his wife as she was when alive, not now.

He walked for about half an hour until he found a huge metal door embedded in a rock wall.

He tried to open it, but it wouldn't budge, and in frustration he kicked and punched and thumped and hit and… until exhausted, he dropped to his knees.

Then the door swung open.

Standing there was an Android. Nearly two metres tall, powerful eyes, that familiar sneer, but fully clothed in a robe and sandals.

Untouched by the madness above? Was that possible?

"Who are you?" its voiced boomed.

"Hob," Hob replied.

"You are a master?"

"I am the last of them. Everyone is dead."

The Android lifted Hob up and brought him into the chamber. High-tech equipment everywhere, the most sophisticated machines imaginable. Hob's eyes settled on a circular table, large enough for him and Takhen to sleep upon.

"That was the idea," he mumbled, wondering if somewhere

"THE MACHINERY CANNOT FAIL. RUK IS THE GUARDIAN OF THE MACHINERY. RUK ENSURES THE MACHINERY CAN NEVER FAIL."

in eternity, Takhen might still hear him. "We were going to create new bodies for ourselves instead of children. Bodies that needed no food, no water, no sleep. Bodies that would not destroy the planet any more through rapacious greed and desire.' Hob laughed and patted the Android guardian's arm. "Instead, my friend, we created you to care for us. The advance guard, the guardians, until we were ready."

The Android seemed to be considering Hob's words. "What do you want me to do, Master?"

Hob stared at the machinery, looking for something, a specific switch he recalled one of the Municipals insisting on. A control only a handful of them even knew had been built. Hob shook his head;

it was getting hard to focus. Was all that he had ensured finally catching up with him?

He found the machinery he needed. It was still lit up, and still active. With a grunt, he slammed his hand onto it.

Hob sighed, it was done, the Androids were deactivated - permanently. The experiment was over.

Hob turned and gasped in astonishment. The guardian Android which had let him in was still standing, head slightly cocked as if trying to work put what had happened. "Either the machinery failed –" Hob started, but was interrupted.

"The machinery cannot fail. Ruk is the guardian of the machinery. Ruk ensures the machinery can never fail."

Hob shrugged. "In that case,

Ruk, we must be so far below ground that the signal I sent out can't penetrate these catacombs. I suggest you never go beyond the cave entrance, or it might deactivate you too."

Hob looked around. "Guard this well, Ruk. One day someone will come. Maybe a survivor from above, from somewhere else on Exo III. One day this equipment may save someone's life."

"It could save yours," Ruk said.

Hob shook his head. "I don't deserve an android body, my friend. Promise me, promise me you'll protect everything here."

"Ruk promises the Master."

"Thank you, Ruk." Hob smiled, closed his eyes… and let the darkness take him for the last time. ✦

The Disavowed

STORY: CHRISTOPHER COOPER

OMMANDER WILLIAM T. RIKER, PERSONAL LOG:

"Counselor Troi's assessment of the political discord on Piivedan was bang on the money: tensions are riding high, to the point where it's hard to imagine either side reaching a compromise, let alone making a joint argument in support of their world's application for admission to the Federation—if they can even agree that's what they really want!

We'll see if anything changes in the next session, but right now I'm inclined to recommend we leave them to settle their differences in their own time."

* * *

Riker shifted in his seat as he listened to the ongoing deposition of Conciliator b'Yornsyn, seemingly designed to muddy the diplomatic waters ever further. He couldn't deny that b'Yornsyn was a skilled orator, and she cast an effortless spell over the massed dignitaries crowded into the debating chamber, but it was beginning to feel like they'd become caught in a temporal loop of argument and counter argument.

He glanced over at Deanna, sat beside Lieutenant Commander Data on the observer's benches, but didn't need her empathic abilities to sense she shared his frustration. Something had to give.

"If I may interrupt," Riker interjected as b'Yornsyn made one of her signature dramatic pauses. The Conciliator glared at the Starfleet officer, clearly taken aback by his unexpected intervention. He fired one of his most disarming grins at her in return.

"Of course, Mediator," she acquiesced after glaring at him a moment longer. Giving him the floor, she'd made it clear she was not happy to do so.

Riker adjusted his uniform tunic and took her place at the center of the chamber. It was time to get things moving. Surely that was the point of installing a Federation outsider as mediator in these proceedings?

"As a member of Starfleet, I've often found myself in situations where people don't see eye to eye," Riker began. He paused, checking that he had his audience's attention. "As mediator in these talks, it's my duty to at least get people facing in the same direction. It isn't my place to lead the discussion, yet we seem to find ourselves at an impasse…"

Was it his imagination, or were the ambassadors from the Amorphan region tidying their papers as if the session was over?

"An impasse that…" He faltered again. Now they were getting up to leave, as were the Relkan Sect, which counted b'Yornsyn as its spiritual head. She was nowhere to be seen.

"If I could have your attention for a moment?" Riker raised his voice, but apparently no one was listening anymore. In fact, the chamber was rapidly emptying, the delegates sharing opinions on the proceedings convivially as they departed. Even Deanna and Data were leaving their seats. Riker hurried over.

"Hey. Where do you two think you are going?" he asked. "The session isn't over. Or did I miss something?"

Neither reacted, and showed no sign they could even see him. Confused, Riker reached out to Deanna—and felt a jolt of shock when his hand passed right through her.

Composing himself, Riker almost instinctively tapped his combadge, welcoming its familiar activation tone. "Riker to *Enterprise*."

No response. He tried again.

"*Enterprise*, this is Commander Riker. Can you hear me?"

Still nothing. Then the sound of Deanna's voice caught his ear.

"Counselor Troi to *Enterprise*. Two to beam up."

"Wait!" Riker protested, but his friends were gone.

* * *

"Welcome back," said Captain Picard as Data and Troi stepped off the transporter pad. He frowned. The away team was missing a member. "Is there a reason Mr. Riker hasn't returned?"

Data looked perplexed. "Mr. Riker, Sir?"

"Yes?" Picard was taken aback by Data's response. He appeared to have never heard the name before.

"I was not aware that a guest would be accompanying us, captain," Data answered.

The captain considered both members of his senior staff, unimpressed. "Is this some kind of joke?" he demanded. His question was met with blank expressions.

Picard looked from Data to Troi and back again. "William Riker," he prompted. "First Officer of the *Enterprise*, and has been for several years."

Troi smiled. "I look forward to meeting him."

For reasons unknown, it appeared that they had no memory of their friend and colleague. Picard began to feel uneasy. "Did anything out of the ordinary happen during the hearing today?" Picard asked.

"Not that I'm aware of," Troi frowned.

"Mr. Data?"

The android tilted his head in the habitual manner that indicated he was accessing his positronic memory. "Nothing that springs to mind captain. Although the Relkan sect's conciliator did end her deposition at a somewhat premature juncture."

"Report directly to Mr. La Forge for a full diagnostic," Picard ordered. "Tell him I want to know if there any gaps or aberrations in your datalog."

"My systems are functioning within normal parameters, sir," Data insisted.

"That's as may be, but I'd like to

be sure." Picard tapped his combadge. "Doctor Crusher, report to Sick Bay. I have a patient for you."

Something was most definitely wrong, and he was beginning to fear the worst. "Computer. What is the current location of Commander Riker?"

"Commander William T. Riker cannot be located."

* * *

Riker cursed under his breath. The sensors that should have detected his proximity and opened the chamber's doors stubbornly refused to acknowledge his presence.

"Come on!" he complained, but the doors remained stubbornly shut. So it wasn't just other people that couldn't see him, it was technology too. In material terms he had ceased to exist, which meant he was trapped inside the chamber, at least until the next session convened. Quite what would happen then, with the appointed mediator rendered wholly intangible, was anyone's guess.

As he considered his next move, Riker heard a faint rumble somewhere in the recesses of the ancient space. Gears rasping as they turned, the scrape of stone against stone. He glanced around, searching for where the noise was coming from, and spied a widening slither of light that split a section of wall. Another entrance? How it had escaped his attention before, Riker couldn't say, but he was glad to see it. He watched as a figure slipped furtively through the gap and hurried across the debating chamber.

"Conciliator b'Yornsyn!" Riker exclaimed. "What have you been up to back there?"

Unsurprisingly she showed no signs of having heard him as she swept through the main doors and into the brightly lit Division Hall beyond. Riker saw his opportunity and went to follow, but a nagging thought caused him to hang back. As enticing as this chance to escape was, he was more intrigued by where b'Yornsyn had come from.

Riker could hear the secret door already grinding shut and came to a decision, darting through the closing

A WIZENED FIGURE STUMBLED OUT FROM BEHIND THE PILLAR AND STAGGERED TOWARDS RIKER.

gap before the mysterious portal disappeared again.

Whatever was back here, he felt sure he would find answers.

* * *

Doctor Beverly Crusher studied the readouts on the biobed scanner above Counselor Troi, and scowled. "There's nothing medically wrong with her," she told the captain. "However, I've found some evidence of increased neurogenesis within Deanna's hippocampus."

"Could that be a normal function of Betazoid biology?" Picard asked.

"I don't think so," replied the doctor. She pointed at sharp nodes of orange light blinking fiercely in the graphic of Troi's brain on the screen. "These new neurons appear to be displacing, bypassing, and in some cases blocking existing synaptic pathways. It's as if a series of roadblocks have been put in place to divert her powers of recollection."

"Which is why I can't remember…" Troi's expression clouded as her mind went blank. "What was his name again?"

"Specifically any memories concerning Will," Crusher confirmed, and she squeezed Troi's hand

reassuringly. "I'll need to run more tests, but I believe the neurons are artificial. I'm not certain they can be removed without causing further memory loss."

"Is he worth remembering?" Deanna asked.

"We'll let you to be the judge of that," answered Picard, exchanging a knowing look with Crusher.

Picard's combadge trilled. "Engineering to Captain Picard," Geordi La Forge's voice emanated from the device.

"Go ahead."

"It's Data, sir. I've never seen anything like it, but…"

"You've discovered artificial neurons blocking Data's memory?" Picard interrupted his chief engineer. "We have an identical case in sick bay. Is the lieutenant commander still with you?"

"He's about to join you now, captain."

"Divert him to Transporter Room 3, and meet us there. It seems Commander Riker may be in need of urgent assistance."

* * *

It took a moment for Riker to adjust to his new surroundings. He was in a tunnel, lit by incandescent orbs.

At the far end was an antechamber, no doubt where b'Yornsyn had been lurking. But what immediately caught his attention were the bodies.

The first was almost identifiable as a humanoid, though more dust than corpse, as Riker discovered when his foot brushed against it and the shape crumbled into nothingness. Despite the gruesome nature of this discovery, he was relieved to feel solid again, and it gave him the confidence to examine the next body more closely.

Despite being in an advanced state of decay, this second cadaver was better preserved, although dressed in robes that suggested it had been lying here for some decades, or even longer. Was this to be his fate too? Riker shuddered at the thought.

"You touched it?"

Riker jumped at the unexpected voice. "Who's there?" he demanded.

"You can hear me? Oh my, are you… are you real?" the voice came again, dry as kindling. A wizened figure stumbled out from behind a pillar and staggered towards Riker, a smile of unbridled joy on his face. Riker caught the old man as his painfully thin legs gave way beneath him.

"I'm real enough," Riker assured the man, gently helping him to sit on the floor. "How long have you been in here?"

"I have no idea," whispered old man. "A week, a month, a year? Not as long as these poor souls, whoever they were. How about you?"

"Too long. My name is William Riker. I'm a Starfleet officer."

"Starfleet!" said the old man, awe and wonder in his tired voice. "So, we've joined the Federation at last."

"Not so much," admitted Riker. "And maybe never, if Conciliator b'Yornsyn continues to prove so… obstructive."

"*Conciliator* b'Yornsyn?" the man asked, his tone suddenly hardened. "So, she even had the gall to take my place. I suppose I shouldn't be surprised. She was against everything I stood for."

"*You* were the Relkan conciliator?" Riker struggled to recall the name of b'Yornsyn's predecessor, a man who had reportedly passed away during the early stages of the planet's quest for Federation membership. "f'Savian, right? You were one of the cosignatories on Piivedan's initial application."

"I was. And it is more than an honor to meet you, Starfleet officer William Riker," f'Savian smiled.

"You said b'Yornsyn took your place. Could she also be responsible for what's happened to me?"

f'Savian nodded. "I uncovered evidence she was plotting a coup with aid from a foreign agent, a Ferengi with deep pockets. When I confronted her, she used the device to banish me. If she's been brazen enough to use it on you, then her plans must be at an advanced stage."

"Back up there—what 'device?'"

"Help me up," said the old man, struggling to get to his feet. "I have something to show you."

Riker supported f'Savian until they reached the antechamber, a space that gave every impression of being dedicated to private worship. A carved altar at its center was decorated with an array of glowing crystals, with a circle of glass-like columns surrounding it. Supporting the antechamber's vaulted ceiling, each column pulsed with energy. It put Riker in mind of the warp core on the *Enterprise*, and he couldn't shake the feeling that they were standing at the heart of a powerful machine.

"Is this a chapel or a control room?" he wondered aloud.

"A device that should have been destroyed a millennia ago," replied f'Savian, his voice heavy with shame. "The historical records insist that it was, yet here it is, fully functional."

"And what exactly is it?"

F'Savian took a deep breath. "A dark stain on the history of my people. This is why you and I are here, how we were stripped of our connection to life. Disavowed."

"This machine did that?" asked Riker in disbelief. "How?"

"Quantum resonance—a technology not dissimilar in concept to your matter transporters," f'Savian explained. "But rather than moving objects from one place to another, this abomination was used by our rulers as the ultimate deterrent for dissention, rephasing the atoms of offenders to a quantum state of existence slightly removed from our reality. The disavowed were damned to

live out what remained of their lives as outsiders, observers, unable to affect any change upon their world."

Riker thought about this. "That explains why my friends couldn't see me, but they should have at least noticed I wasn't there."

"Objectively speaking, that was the subtle beauty of the punishment. The resonator didn't merely shift atoms, it propagated a neurological response in all those present in the main chamber. The accused were not only removed from reality, they were forgotten altogether."

"You mean the debating chamber is part of the device?"

"Oh yes. You'll have noted it's unusual conical internal structure? It focused and defused the quantum wave to every point in the chamber."

"So, you're saying that the democratic process we've been undertaking took place in a room where someone who knew about the existence of this thing could alter the memories of everyone involved?" Riker was stunned by the implications. "No wonder the debate has been in deadlock for so long."

"Oh…" murmured f'Savian,

catching up. "Oh my! b'Yornsyn?"

Riker nodded. "We need to get out of here and stop her."

f'Savian gulped. "In our condition? Good luck with that!"

* * *

Picard and his away team had been searching the debating chamber for fifteen minutes before b'Yornsyn stormed in, followed by a squad of Relkan enforcers.

"What is the meaning of this?" she fumed as she approached the captain. "How dare you enter this sacred place without permission? This is precisely the kind of authoritarian disregard for sovereignty that I would expect from the Federation's military mafia!"

"Enough hyperbole, Conciliator," said Picard, forcefully. "We're searching for a missing member of my crew, and we have permission from the Arbiter's office to be here. Do you?" b'Yornsyn gritted her teeth. "As Relkan Conciliator, I have every right to ensure due process is adhered to. What is wrong with her?"

The conciliator pointed towards Troi, who was transfixed by a blank

TROI HALTED WHEN [RIKER] CALLED HER NAME, CAUSING HER HEART TO SKIP A BEAT.

wall on the far side of the chamber, Data at her side.

Picard turned his back on b'Yornsyn and addressed Troi. "Counselor?"

"I sense… something familiar," she said, and walked towards the wall.

"Is your crewmember unhinged?" b'Yornsyn demanded, attempting to place herself between Troi and the anonymous section of wall.

"Far from it. Please move aside," Picard commanded. b'Yornsyn grudgingly complied.

Troi touched the stone surface. "Behind here," she said.

Data raised his tricorder and scanned the blank wall. "A door," he stated, reaching out to touch a sigil carved into the surface. With a barely audible grind, the door slid aside.

"Fascinating," said Data. Without hesitation he stepped through into the tunnel beyond, followed by Troi. Picard let b'Yornsyn to enter ahead of him, aware of her shocked expression.

"Did you know this was here?" he asked.

"No idea," she said, hurrying after the others. Picard detected a strong note of falsehood in her answer.

* * *

"How did you open the door?" f'Savian asked, bewildered.

"I didn't. They found it," said Riker, still shaken by having had Data walk straight through him. Then he understood.

"Deanna!"

Troi halted the moment he said her name, causing his heart to skip a beat. She couldn't hear him, he knew that, but was another connection at play?

"What do we do now?" wondered f'Savian.

"What else can we do?" said Riker. "We watch and see what happens. Come on."

Following Deanna into the antechamber, Riker observed the readings on Data's tricorder as he scanned the altar.

"Crystalline processors. Although I cannot determine its function, this is more than a religious artifact," Data told the others.

"Could it be related to the effects we've encountered?" asked Picard.

With nothing else to lose, and with as much force as he could

muster, Riker shouted, "Yes!" He stared at Deanna, praying desperately for some response. A frown was his reward.

"Captain, I get a strong feeling that is the case," Troi said.

Picard turned to b'Yornsyn. "You know what this does?"

"Me? No, how could I?"

"She's lying," Troi and Riker said in unison.

"What? How dare you…" b'Yornsyn responded, flustered. Then she noticed Data was manipulating the crystals on the altar. "No, don't touch those!" she shouted and moved to push him out of the way.

"Don't move," Picard commanded, his phaser aimed at the wild-eyed conciliator. "What have you done with my first officer?"

"I'm right here, Sir," Riker's disembodied voice echoed around the chamber, as two shadowy masses began to flicker into existence, silhouetted against the flickering, fading lights of the pillars.

"Will!" Deanna cried out, and rushed to embrace him. Riker appreciated the warmth of her body against his more keenly than ever. ⚶

Paghabi

STORY: CHRIS DOWS
ILLUSTRATION: LOUIE DE MARTINIS

"Doctor Crusher to the fencing room. Medical emergency!"

Picard knelt beside the shuddering form of Guinan, prying the foil from her vice-like grip. In all his years of knowing the El-Aurian, he had never seen her stumble, let alone collapse as she just had. Something was *very* wrong here, and as if to reinforce his fears, the *Enterprise* lurched violently, knocking him off-balance as the airy room was bathed in a scarlet glow.

"All hands, red alert. Captain Picard to the bridge."

Guinan's convulsions increased, her eyes wide and white in the back of her head.

"Number one, report."

"It's best you see for yourself, Captain. It's a little hard to describe."

A thunderous rumble shook the *Enterprise*, heralding the arrival of Doctor Beverly Crusher and Nurse Ogawa who stumbled through the entrance doors. One look at Jean-Luc's face, and Crusher knew things were serious.

"What happened?"

Rising, Picard straightened his uniform and looked down at his friend with a sigh.

"She… fell. That's all I can tell you, Doctor."

Crusher ran her tricorder over Guinan's shaking body and looked up with a frown. "We need to get her to sickbay. And you need to get to the bridge."

With a nod, Picard strode out of the room.

* * *

Entering the bridge and striding to the conn, Picard studied the extraordinary scene on the viewscreen, signaling Riker to mute the red alert klaxon as he passed his first officer.

"Data, what am I looking at here?"

Data turned to face his captain.

"It appears to be a rift in the space-time continuum. Emissions from the fissure have overwhelmed sensors and long-range communications. I am attempting to recalibrate to gather further data."

Picard stared at the swirling maelstrom of color framed by the ragged slash of normal space. He'd seen fractures in the continuum before, but nothing as vibrant and energetic as this. A brilliant pulse of light flashed across the bridge, causing the ship to shake again. Worf's gruff voice boomed from behind Picard's command position.

"Object detected on the boundaries of the rift, Captain."

Out of his peripheral vision, Picard saw Troi rise from her seat to his left. Leaning forwards, he focused on the single point of pulsating light which scurried frantically between the opposing sides of the widening tear.

"What is it, Data?"

Data's fingers became a blur on his station's controls. He allowed himself a frown to mimic frustration.

"Unknown, sir. Sensors are barely operational, but it possesses a massive energy signature and a significant level of electromagnetic radiation across all spectrums."

Riker looked up from his screen, his eyes narrowing as he watched the object increase in speed around the opening rift and shared the observation he'd made with the bridge.

"Its movement isn't random. There's a pattern emerging, which suggests intelligence."

A huge shockwave hit the ship, knocking Troi back into her seat and Worf off his feet at his security station. Retaking his position, the Klingon spoke with urgency as waves of energy continued to batter the *Enterprise*.

"What if it is the cause of the rift? The phenomenon is increasing in size, matching the direction of the object."

Data turned again from his console.

"I am detecting building inverse graviton emissions which are already threatening our ability to go to warp. If the rupture continues to expand at this rate, it could destabilize this entire sector."

As Picard weighed up the mounting threat, Worf voiced what many were reluctantly thinking.

"Recommend we neutralize the object to prevent the rift spreading further."

Troi looked to Picard, concern etched in her face.

"Captain, I'm not comfortable attacking an entity we know so little about. Can we not attempt to communicate with it?"

Picard looked to Data, who shook his head.

"All comms are still unavailable."

Picard took in a breath and exhaled, using the brief time to consider the situation. It might be the only chance they get to stop the rift's progression and keep his crew safe.

"I agree with your sentiments Counselor but given the level of threat facing us, we have to act on the limited information in our possession. Lieutenant Worf – target the object with a low yield photon torpedo. Let's try to disable rather than destroy it."

Worf indicated readiness and, with a heavy heart, Picard gave the order to fire. The bridge fell silent save for the increasingly powerful impacts from the fissure's energy waves as the crew watched the torpedo streak towards the energetic object. It detonated with a flash, extinguishing the light from the object and immediately halting the turbulence. But then, a low frequency hum vibrated through the ship, escalating rapidly in frequency and volume to

WITH A HEAVY HEART, PICARD GAVE THE ORDER TO FIRE.

a deafening squeal. Everyone but Data clutched the sides of their head to stifle the sound. Abruptly the sound stopped, only to be replaced by the screams of Deanna Troi who, overwhelmed by some unseen force, twisted in pain then slumped back into her chair, unconscious.

Shaking off his disorientation, Riker staggered to his feet and over to the counselor as Picard ordered a situation report. Data's need to re-initialize the now completely overwhelmed scanners meant he couldn't immediately assess the situation. Worf's confirmation the object had been deactivated by the torpedo was interrupted by a message at his security station.

"Crusher to bridge. Guinan has left sickbay. She's not - "

Another communication came in, overriding the doctor's terse voice.

"Bridge, this is transporter room one. I have Guinan here and she's - "

The sound of a struggle could be heard, then the channel closed as a warning flashed on Worf's console.

"Captain, someone is attempting to activate the transporter."

Head still spinning from the cacophony, Picard forced himself to his feet.

"*What?* Override."

Worf moved fast, but not fast enough.

"Transport in progress sir… to the location of the object."

Picard's stomach lurched. It had to be Guinan.

"Number one, get the Counselor to sickbay. Data – get those sensors back online. We need to know if the rift's stop spreading. Worf – you're with me."

* * *

Picard entered transporter room one before the doors had fully opened. Before him, the pad was dimmed to standby. Striding to the control interface, he ignored the groans of the technician on the floor, directing Worf to see to him while Picard studied the readouts. He estimated she'd been in space, presumably unprotected, for over two minutes, well past the limit most humanoids could expect to survive.

He had to hope El-Aurians had a little more resilience to the harshness of space.

The interference on the telemetry systems was considerable from the rift's emissions, so Picard used Guinan's inputted coordinates and hoped neither of them had moved. The transporter pad shimmered into life and as the cycle began, but alarms winked on to show a lock couldn't be maintained without more power. Picard boosted the signal to maximum and, after a few tense seconds, an outline shimmered into existence at the front of the circular dais.

"Captain!"

Worf's shouted warning came a split second after Picard's realization this wasn't the familiar form he'd hoped to see. Guinan pulsed with the same brilliant aura as the object, eyes closed and head tilted back as if she were looking to the sky. Glancing down at the controls, Picard could see a mismatch with the pattern buffers.

Something was inside her.

Picard activated an emergency forcefield around the frozen form, the barrier fizzing in time with the

light radiating from Guinan's body. As the technician rose unsteadily on his feet, Worf joined Picard at the control station, checking for toxic levels of radiation in the room or other dangers.

"Picard to sickbay."

"Crusher here."

"Doctor, we have retrieved Guinan but she has been… invaded by some unknown presence."

"Give me a few seconds to set up a quarantine field then beam her directly here."

"Understood."

By the time Picard entered sickbay, Doctor Crusher was well into her scans of Guinan from outside the glowing containment field surrounding the surgical table. On one of the nearby treatment beds, Troi lay unconscious, watched over by nurse Ogawa with care and intent. Crusher moved over to the main diagnostic screen on the opposing wall to Troi's position. It displayed a real-time map of Guinan's central nervous system.

"Doctor. Report."

Crusher glanced over to Picard with a frown.

"Some entity has incorporated itself into Guinan's body and is feeding off her electro-chemical emissions."

This confirmed Picard's worst fears. The mysterious object they had attacked without provocation was a living being, one they had never previously encountered. His heart fell, but there was no point in regret; he had made the decision based on the information available at the time, and now he had to deal with the consequences. Through the field, Picard saw the distorted form of Doctor Crusher turn to Guinan's glowing body.

"One thing I can't understand is Guinan's reaction to this parasite. She doesn't seem to be putting up any kind of fight. And I don't know how long she can withstand this drain on her energy, Jean-Luc."

Picard walked around the perimeter of the field, trying to think through the situation. His attempts to make sense of it were rudely interrupted by his communicator.

"Riker to Captain Picard. Sensors are back online and Data reports the rift is continuing to expand at a faster rate than before. Comms are still out so we cannot alert Starfleet Command of the situation."

Picard studied Guinan. Her hands were folded across her abdomen, and she had a look of strange contentment on her face.

"Understood, number one. Stand by."

Picard nodded to himself. Things were starting to connect.

"Doctor, could it be the entity is using Guinan to recover from our attack?"

Crusher raised an eyebrow and considered the suggestion.

"It's certainly a possibility, but why Guinan?"

Picard regarded his old friend. There were so many things he didn't know about her, yet they shared a bond of understanding exclusive to his associations.

"El-Aurians have a unique relationship with the space-time continuum. It cannot be a coincidence Guinan collapsed just before this situation arose, nor would Guinan have acted as she did without extraordinary reason."

"True, but what if her El-Aurian characteristics made her the most viable and attractive host, and the entity coerced her somehow? It must have protected her from the vacuum to ensure its host survived."

An alarm sounded, and the display showing Guinan's nervous system turned red. On the table, Guinan's faint smile changed into a grimace of pain, her knuckles white with the intensity of her grasp.

"Vital signs are plummeting. She's going to arrest if I don't intervene immediately."

Nurse Ogawa quickly rose from Troi's bedside to assist the Doctor. Picard's communicator sounded again.

"Captain, engineering reports we can no longer generate a warp envelope in this area of space."

The edge in Riker's voice told Picard everything he needed to know.

"Get us out of here, number one. Full impulse."

Crusher manipulated the medical screen interface. On the surgical bed, a cowling slid into place over Guinan's chest.

"There's no evidence of any exterior contamination but if the life-form decides to jump ship into me, on no account drop the containment field. I'm going in."

Before Picard or Ogawa had time to protest, Crusher passed through the barrier and began working on Guinan. The large screen started to flash warning signs on Guinan's schematic, and Crusher looked directly to Picard with a grim expression.

"The entity has coalesced into a concentrated form at the base of her brain stem. I can target it with a pulse of ultrasound and destroy it."

Picard glanced over to Guinan's vital signs, all of which were flattening out.

"Will it save her?"

Crusher reached for a handheld emitter from a nearby tray and fine-tuned its controls.

"If I don't kill the creature, she will certainly die, given these readings."

And there it was. A classic *Kobayashi Maru*. Did Picard attempt to save his friend and eradicate a

> "DOCTOR, WE HAVE RETRIEVED GUINAN BUT SHE HAS BEEN… INVADED BY SOME UNKNOWN PRESENCE."

potentially unique life-form, or leave it to consume Guinan and create a situation with yet more unknown factors? Neither option was attractive, but he had to decide regardless.

"Proceed, Doctor."

Crusher nodded and moved to Guinan's head, gently moving it to one side then activating the small device. Bringing it into contact with the base of Guinan's neck, Crusher took a breath and moved her thumb to activate the beam.

"STOP!"

All heads snapped to Deanna Troi, who was sitting bolt upright on the treatment bed, a pleading hand outstretched.

"Beverly, please, leave Guinan alone. She is in no danger."

Crusher looked to the readings on the medical screen. All of Guinan's life-signs were plateauing.

"Deanna, whatever this thing is, it's killing Guinan."

"I have a telepathic link to Guinan through the entity. She tells me she has willingly allowed

paghabi to feed from her, and that it will not take her life. It is no threat to us either, Captain. All it needs is sustenance to complete the task we interrupted."

Picard threw a glance to Crusher, who stood hesitantly with the emitter in hand, then moved towards Troi, still wary of the unfolding events.

"Explain, Counselor."

Troi spoke calmly, in her usual warm, measured tones.

"*Paghabi* exist to repair natural tears in the fabric of the universe. They share an ancient, deep bond with El-Aurians, who help them in their work when called upon. It's the remnants of a symbiotic relationship that stretches back eons. As soon as it has recovered, it will return to its work and mend the rift on its own – but the longer it stays here, the longer the restoration will take."

As Troi finished her explanation, the indicators stopped flashing on Guinan's readouts, her life-signs beginning a gradual crawl to normal. Crusher stepped back from her patient, placed the emitter back on the tray and deactivated the containment field as Picard turned to her.

"Doctor, you mentioned *paghabi* is feeding off electro-chemical energy from Guinan. Is there any way you can help accelerate the healing process?"

Crusher thought for a second then nodded.

"I could isolate the energy frequency and generate a concentrated dose. I'd have to work through Deanna to ensure I got the feed right, but it could work."

Picard looked to Guinan, who now had a faint smile on her lips.

"Picard to bridge. Number one – reverse course, best speed to the rift."

"Captain?"

Riker's voice was incredulous.

"I'll explain everything in a few minutes Will. For now, carry out my orders."

"Aye, sir."

Picard walked over to Guinan and placed his hand gently on hers.

"Contact me as soon as *paghabi* is recovered enough to leave the ship Doctor. I've got a lot of questions to ask… and some apologizing to do."

"*Pulaski 2.0*"

STORY: GREG COX

octor Katherine Pulaski, chief medical officer of the U.S.S. *Enterprise,* stared at herself in the mirror provided by her welcoming committee. She looked much as she should, right down to her curly blonde hair, blue Starfleet uniform, and shiny gold communicator badge, but she felt . . . off. She rubbed her fingers together, relieved to discover, as promised, sufficient tactile sensation, but the rest of her felt oddly unfamiliar. Then she realized what was missing: she had no heartbeat, no pulse, nor any of the usual aches and pains that flesh was heir to, even in this day and age.

So this is what it's like to be an android, she thought.

* * *

Hours earlier:

"In short," Captain Picard briefed his senior officers in the ship's spacious conference room, "Lloua III, an independent planetoid outside the Federation's borders, is essentially a 24th-century leper colony, housing individuals who are carriers of *malefic dementia*, an incurable virus that presently resists all known means of containment, including environmental suits, transporter biofilters, and so on. The virus induces madness and death for most who contract it, and any survivors remain extremely contagious for the rest of their lives. As a result, no one who visits Lloua III can ever be allowed to leave, for fear of spreading the disease."

"How dreadful," Troi remarked. "Hard to imagine that such places are still needed in our time."

"I assure you, Counselor, our colony is no dismal hellhole." Nae Yemma, an apprentice physician on Lloua III, addressed them via a viewscreen. She was a humanoid, whose youthful features boasted a slightly iridescent complexion. "It's very clean and comfortable, with a pleasant climate and every civilized amenity. Our lives are full, satisfying, and relatively carefree . . . at least until the present crisis."

According to Yemma, the colony's resident doctor and surgeon, one Jale Yaslo, had been badly injured in what was believed to be a freak laboratory accident. He was in desperate need of an artificial heart transplant, which no one else on the colony was qualified to perform. This was all more the more urgent given that Yaslo was possibly on the verge of curing the virus at long last. With the *Enterprise* responding to an urgent distress signal, Pulaski was the only surgeon in the sector who can possibly save Yaslo but how could she operate on the patient without getting infected – and carrying the virus back to the *Enterprise?*

"We may have a solution," Yemma continued. "As you may be aware, our people are descended – very distantly – from an ancient star-faring race, long extinct, who once aspired to implant their disembodied consciousnesses into new android bodies. I believe your own Federation once encountered the last remnants of that bygone civilization."

"Sargon's people," Pulaski said, nodding. She had reviewed that incident, as documented in Starfleet's medical database by the pioneering work of Doctor Ann Mulhall, in the wake of Ira Graves' attempt to hijack Data's body a few months ago. She understood that, in the decades since Kirk's *Enterprise* had discovered Sargon and his cohorts, Starfleet had confirmed that various remote alien peoples were indeed descended from those ancient explorers. "So what exactly do you propose?"

"We have the means, Doctor, to temporarily beam your mind into an android duplicate of your body, which you can use to perform the operation. Afterwards, we can transfer your mind back to your actual body on the *Enterprise,* so there is never any chance of you contracting or spreading the infection."

Pulaski blanched. To say that the prospect of becoming an android, even temporarily, was disturbing was the understatement of the century. "What about the android's own mind?" she asked, recalling Grave's selfish usurpation of Data's form. She had no desire to commit the same crime.

"Our androids lack any truly sophisticated positronic brains; they're simply empty shells with no genuine artificial intelligence."

"That is reassuring," Data observed. "Speaking from experience, it is unsettling to have another personality downloaded into one's circuitry."

Pulaski eyed him wryly. "You're enjoying this, aren't you, Data?"

"I do not comprehend, Doctor. I am not capable of having any feelings on the matter."

"Never mind." She should have learned by now that bantering with Data was a lost cause. He was altogether too sincere and innocent to give as good as he got.

"Well, Doctor?" Picard asked. "This is entirely your choice. I cannot in good conscience order you to undergo this procedure."

"Needless to say, I'm not thrilled by the idea, but I don't see another option." She sighed in resignation. "Sometimes my Hippocratic Oath can be a damned pain in the rear."

* * *

Down on Lloua III, Pulaski had little time to adjust to her new body. Beyond the severity of her patient's condition, there was another ticking clock involved; apparently her consciousness had to be returned to her actual body within approximately six hours or her physical form back on the *Enterprise* would begin to fail. What's more, she'd been informed that her mind could not survive indefinitely within its temporary cybernetic brain before it began to degrade. In short, she needed to operate on Yaslo, and put her mind back where it belonged, pronto.

"Don't worry," Yemma assured her. "We'll get you back to this station as soon we can."

The mind-transfer apparatus was located in an impressively state-of-the-art lab within a larger municipal complex. Pulaski glimpsed clear skies, swaying trees, and an inviting lakefront through tinted picture windows as Yemma escorted her to a medical facility a few floors below the transfer station. She memorized the route in case she needed to retrace it in a hurry.

Another colonist, short and fidgety, greeted them outside the entrance to the operating room. Yemma introduced him as Rugin, Doctor Yaslo's lab assistant. Pulaski noted what appeared to be freshly restored tissue on the man's shaved pate, still looking very slick and pristine. He carried himself somewhat gingerly as well.

"Rugin was slightly injured in the same explosion that nearly killed Yaslo," Yemma explained. "Thankfully, no major surgery was required."

THE OPERATION WAS PROVING MORE COMPLICATED, NOT TO MENTION TIME-CONSUMING THAN ANTICIPATED.

Pulaski was glad to have only one patient in critical condition. "About that explosion, any idea what caused it?"

"That remains under investigation, although" – Yemma hesitated before continuing – "it seems there's now some concern that it might *not* have been an accident after all."

"Oh?" Pulaski was troubled to hear this, belatedly. "Do tell."

Rugin looked uncomfortable. "I hate to point fingers, but Yaslo had begun acting . . . erratically . . . just prior to the explosion. Violent mood swings, from euphoria to despair, sometimes in the space of minutes." He wrung his hands together. "Perhaps the virus finally affected his brain, even after so many years?"

Pulaski could not rule out the possibility. Such delayed symptomology among carriers was rare, but not unprecedented. "What's your take on this?" she asked Yemma.

"Frankly, that's beyond my purview. My only concern right now is treating our patient."

"Quite right," Pulaski conceded. She was here to operate on Yaslo, not play detective. "Let's get to it."

"Will he be all right?" Rugin asked anxiously as they left him behind in the waiting area. He seemed desperate for an answer. "Can you save him?"

"I'll do my best," she promised.

* * *

"As a Vulcan," Doctor Selar informed Picard in sickbay, "I have some familiarity with the concept of *katra* transference, but I must warn you that performing a full *fal-tor-pan* ritual is quite beyond my capabilities. I'm a physician, not an adept."

Selar monitored Pulaski's inert body via the illuminated displays above the biobed. A helmet-like device, replicated from patterns transmitted from the colony, cradled Pulaski's head. The helmet was merely a receiver/transmitter, operated remotely from the main control room and mechanism on Lloua III.

"In other words," Picard

translated, "you cannot telepathically restore Pulaski's mind to her body on your own, but must rely on the technology down on the planetoid."

"Precisely."

* * *

"I'm not liking these enzyme readings," Yemma reported, assisting in the operation. "They're sliding way out of balance."

"Increase the amplitude of the cardiostimulator," Pulaski said, frowning. Her artificial hands kept busy beneath the surgical support frame mounted over Yaslo's unconscious form. An overhead unit projected a sterile field. "We need to get those numbers stabilized before we go any further."

The operation was proving more complicated, not to mention time-consuming, than anticipated. On the positive side, Pulaski noted, her android body did not suffer from fatigue, hunger, or thirst, allowing her to operate steadily without a break. Nor did she need a nurse on hand to

[PULASKI] WASN'T SURE SHE COULD PANIC IF SHE WANTED TO.

wipe any sweat from her synthetic brow. On the other hand, she was all too acutely aware that time was slipping away. At this rate, she was going to be calling it close to get back to her own body before it was too late.

Not that she could ever walk out on a patient during surgery.

"Pass me that tissue mitigator, stat!"

* * *

"Her life-signs are weakening, Captain," Selar reported, concern showing through her stoic demeanor. "I've applied certain Vulcan therapies to bolster her autonomic nervous system, but there is a limit to their effectiveness. Her *katra* needs to be restored to her physical being in a timely fashion if either are to survive."

"Understood, Doctor."

Last Picard had heard, the operation was still underway. He felt singularly helpless, unable even to beam down to monitor the situation personally. Everything was in the doctors' hands now.

Both of them.

* * *

"There! That should do it."

Pulaski completed the cardiac replacement with scant minutes to spare. Glancing at a chronometer, she saw that she needed to get to the mind-transfer station right away.

"Go!" Yemma said. "I can finish up here!"

"You don't have to tell me twice."

Pulaski didn't bother to shed her surgical scrubs before dashing out of the operating room to discover that Rugin was still waiting just outside the chamber. Had he been here this whole time, anxious to hear how the surgery went?

"Did you do it? Is he going to live?"

"Looks like it," she said briskly, trying to squeeze past him, "but if you'll excuse me—"

"No! He mustn't survive. I can't let that happen!"

He threw open a rumpled lab coat to reveal a crude-looking, jury-rigged device strapped to his chest. Bloodshot eyes, practically bulging from their sockets, gleamed with madness. Spittle sprayed from his lips.

"It was you," Pulaski realized. "You blew up the lab before."

"Don't you see, I had no choice.

Finding a cure means the end of the colony. This is our home. I can't let him destroy it!"

Pulaski understood now. The virus, long dormant in his system, had driven Rugin mad, not Yaslo. "Listen to me, you're not thinking clearly--"

"You don't understand! He can't survive! I won't allow it!" He glanced down at his chest. "Activate self-destruct!"

The improvised suicide vest responded to his voice command. Indicator lights flashed ominously. A high-pitched whine, like a hand phaser on overload, issued from the device. Rugin started toward the operating room – where Yemma and Yaslo were defenseless against the demented lab tech and his bomb.

"Out of my way, Doctor!"

"Not a chance."

She was surprised by how cool and collected she felt, considering, then recalled that she presently lacked any adrenal glands to trigger a fight-or-flight response. She wasn't sure she could panic if she wanted to. And, come to think of it, it wasn't as though her *real* body was in jeopardy from the bomb.

Let's put this polyalloy carcass to the test . . . .

She tackled Rugin to keep him away from the operating room, hoping the android body would take the brunt of the explosion. He fought to throw her off, but was outmatched by her superior weight and strength.

"Bomb!" she shouted to any colonists who might be in earshot. "Run!"

Was there a chance to defuse the device, she wondered, right before the rising whine was cut off by a deafening thunderclap. An intense flare temporarily whited out her vision, even as the heat and force of the blast knocked her offline.

* * *

Rebooting moments later, her fingers felt like they were on fire, but only her fingers. She was suddenly grateful that the android's builders had prioritized manual dexterity at the expense of her other senses. Looking around, she saw that the waiting area was now rubble and that

Rugin had been blown to pieces. A fallen ceiling beam pinned her to the cratered floor, forcing her to exert all her mechanical strength to heave it off her. Straining servomotors hissed and squeaked in protest. Shredded bioplast "flesh" exposed blinking circuitry and glimpses of scorched steel armature. All trace of her scrubs had been burned away.

I've looked better, she guessed.

The android her had survived the blast, but only just. Mangled, shedding sparks and bleeding lubricant, she staggered to her feet and limped away from the blast site and down a painfully endless corridor. Alarms, smoke, and scattered debris marked her progress. An elevator proved inoperative, possibly due to emergency protocols, forcing her to take the stairs instead. The transfer station, two floors above her, seemed light-years away . . . .

* * *

"I'm losing her, Captain."

Selar applied another hypospray to Pulaski's throat, but her somber tone conveyed little hope. A mind-meld was apparently out of the question, given that Pulaski's mind was elsewhere. "*Katra* and body must be rejoined."

Picard tapped his communicator badge urgently. "Picard to Pulaski, please respond." In theory, the colonists had replicated a communicator for Pulaski's use on the planetoid, but the *Enterprise* had been unable to reach her for some time, and now they were receiving word of an explosion at colony's medical facility, although the details were maddeningly *ADJ. "Picard to Pulaski, where the devil are you?"

"No need to shout, Captain. I'm right here."

The figure on the bed blinked and sat up cautiously, as though not entirely trusting her own body. She reached to remove the transfer helmet.

"And, honestly, my head is killing me."

* * *

"I am curious, Doctor," Data said. "How did your find your experience?"

At Selar's insistence, Pulaski was taking it easy in sickbay, where she'd been pleased to hear that Yaslo had made a full recovery and was indeed closing in on a cure for *malefic dementia.* A shame that cure had come too late for Rugin.

"Well, I can't say I'm not relieved to be flesh-and-blood again," she told Data, who had called on her during her convalescence, "but it *was* illuminating to walk a while in your shoes, however briefly. I only hope that someday you'll have the opportunity to do the same in reverse, by achieving your goal of becoming more human."

"Thank you, Doctor, I appreciate the sentiment."

"You're welcome. And, Data, feel free to remind me of this incident the next time I underestimate you, simply because you're an android."

"You may rely on it, Doctor."

Pulaski grinned. "That's the spirit, Data. There may be hope for you yet." ⊀

The Expert

STORY: GARY RUSSELL
ILLUSTRATION: LOUIE DE MARTINIS

Max Thomssen knew things were bad, because everything was dark. Life aboard a starship was never dark. There were always bright lights and glows.

Right now, there wasn't even a flash from the comms unit on the wall or the reassuring glow from the food replicator over by the table. Everything was in total blackness.

He could feel his kid sister squirming against him. She was scared, and didn't want to be there. She wanted to be with Dad. Max didn't blame her, but he knew it was his job to look after her right now.

"It's going to be fine," he whispered to her, "If it's going to be fine," Tori hissed back, "why are we whispering?"

"That's a good point, well made," was the best Max could come back with.

"Where's Dad gone?" Tori mumbled.

Max looked up at the door, wishing he knew the answer. Or at least had an answer that would reassure Tori. He needed to distract her, calm her down. He'd seen Dad do that often enough.

"Look, see, on the table. When he came off-shift earlier, he got The Project out. We were planning to do some more work on it tonight."

"Stupid Project," Tori muttered, 'You're *always* doing stupid Projects."

Max knew she was only really unimpressed by the "Projects" because she realized that each time Dad got it onto the table, it meant it was her bedtime. That was the great thing about being fourteen now, Max thought. He didn't have to go to bed when eleven-year-olds did.

"You should just use relocators," Tori said.

"That's hardly the point, "replied Max, gradually moving towards the Project, which meant Tori had to move, too. He'd got her mind off the darkness. He could almost hear his dad saying that, right now, Max had to be the adult in the room.

"This time, we're building a scale model of the *Lalo*," he said. "Together. Out of materials we can get from aboard the ship. A model of the ship, made by actual parts from the ship, is fun."

Tori was staring at it. "I can see the insides. That's... weird." She looked at her brother with a small smile. "You're weird, too."

She was clearly feeling better. "It's called a skeletal model," Max started to explain. "You can see the insides, because I know everything about this ship. I've studied all the specs of the *Lalo*, well, all the Mediterranean class ships, and -"

"You've missed a bit. There, I can see through to the other side..."

Max nodded. "That's because as we were doing this, I realized the Mediterranean class ships have a design flaw." He felt Tori tense. "Not a bad one," he quickly added. "Just an incidental one, one that doesn't really matter. You see the junction where the conduits on Deck 8 meet the conduits on Deck 9?"

Tori shook her head, but Max pushed on. "The structural integrity is weaker but only needs a slight adjustment and –"

"Like I said. *Weird*."

And with that, Tori went and sat on the floor by the door, looking out into the dark corridor. And shivered. "I wish Mom was here."

Max sighed. He did too, but Lori had been a bit too young to clearly remember the holiday on Risa.

Before ... well, whatever had happened. Max didn't understand either to be truthful, but they had come away from Risa without their family intact, and now only saw Mom twice a year.

As he and Dad had started work on the model of the *Lalo* a few weeks back, it had crossed Max's mind for the first time that Dad still wore the wedding band with its Celtic inscription. He wondered if Mom still wore hers. He'd check next time he saw her.

"Did I tell you about the time I heard Dad tell Chief Engineer P'uruss about that? He was really interested too. Dad took me to meet him, and I explained that I knew pretty much everything about most starships. From the Galaxies and Ambassadors to freight-carriers like the *Lalo*. Dad told him

I could probably find every bulkhead junction and conduit interface aboard the *Lalo* with my eyes shut."

"And can you?"

"Course."

"Show off."

"Dad even told him about my concerns about the integrity of the bulkheads on Decks 8 and 9 to Chief Engineer P'uruss."

"What did she say?"

Max was going to exaggerate, but Tori wasn't stupid, she'd see through that. "She said she'd look into it and that I should carry on my studies."

Tori laughed. "Hah, you mean you got ignored."

Max didn't mind, Lori was laughing for the first time since she'd been woken up by the same thing that had sent Dad back to his science station on Deck 6 - a message demanding all duty officers to report to their stations. Seconds later, the red alert sirens had gone off and Max could feel the ship had gone to high warp with a real jerk. Dad had grabbed his hand, given it a strong squeeze as he'd said 'I better go see what's going on, back soon. Stay here and look after your sister."

And Dad had dashed away.

Max could still feel the slight pressure of that wedding band against his own small fingers. Max wasn't silly enough to believe in things science couldn't prove, yet something instinctively told him this wasn't a training exercise. He couldn't hear any chatter on the comms unit, meaning everyone was either keeping very quiet, which was unlikely, or only using secure channels, keeping information away from the lower decks and civilians aboard.

And then the lights had gone out. Not with a flicker, not even with

an electrical bang, they'd just – gone off.

And sleepy Tori had toppled over, as something seemed to stop the ship in mid-warp, and brought it to a sudden stop. Max wondered if they'd hit anything, but no decompression warnings were sounding; no cold, calm computer voice telling everyone not to worry, and therefore making them both worry ten times more.

Instead, it was dark, cold and silent. The doors jammed open onto the corridor outside.

"It's getting cold," Tori said now, bringing Max back into the moment.

"Yeah," he agreed, but didn't add that he suspected that meant things like life support were starting to be given a lower priority. Something big had to be happening.

"Perhaps we hit something in space. Like an asteroid," Tori said.

Max shrugged. "Maybe".

"We should find Dad."

"He'll be busy," said Max, but realized Tori needed to think reassuring things. So he glanced over at the scale model of the *Lalo* on the tabletop, and closed his eyes, mentally

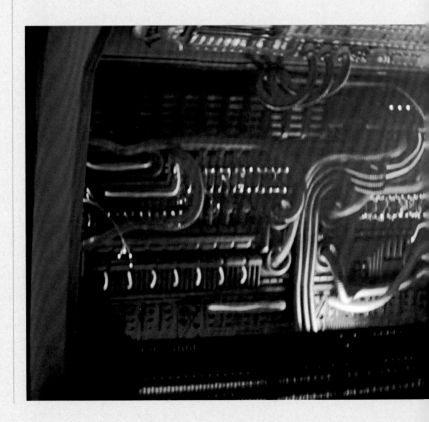

SUDDENLY TORI SQUEALED AS ANOTHER JOLT SHOOK THE SHIP. AND MAX KNEW WHAT THAT WAS – THE LALO WAS FIRING ITS PHASERS.

travelling through the ship they had built so accurately, so precisely. They were on Deck 12. His father would be on Deck 6. And there, between them, Max's pet project: "the weaknesses in the plating on Decks 8 and 9 due to the inclusion of too many conduits meeting at the same point on both decks which weakens both the floors and bulkheads of the decks," as he had told Chief P'uruss.

This wasn't a problem on most of the other classifications of Starfleet ships, because they had their nacelles above not below the main structure. But when building so many models of different ships and space stations over the past few years, Max had realized that the Mediterranean class ships had this unique limitation.

Max couldn't actually prove that it was the position of the nacelles that caused the potential stress fracture, but

it was a project he wanted to explore more. Although it puzzled Max that the new *California*-class ships, which also had lower nacelles, didn't seem to replicate the fault, which meant it could be something else.

Suddenly Tori squealed as another jolt shook the ship. And Max knew what that was – the *Lalo* was firing its phasers.

Why?

Max told Tori they should head to their father's workstation now. Tori agreed, saying she didn't feel safe trapped in the quarters anymore.

Max gave one last look at in the model of the *Lalo*. One last chance to memorize all the corridors and junctions and turbolift shafts.

The corridor was dark, but now he could hear sounds, most of which were distant bangs. Then a flash of white and yellow from around a

corner and Max felt something rush through his body. Adrenaline. But fear? Excitement? Bewilderment? He pushed those questions down and moved towards the light source, gently encouraging Tori all the time, always making sure she was safe.

As they reached the end of the corridor at a T-junction, Max realized it was a plasma fire, a breach on the corridor wall was pumping hot plasma everywhere, so he led Tori in the opposite direction.

This would lead to turbolift J – and an emergency stairwell. Never use the lifts in an emergency, Dad had always said.

A door was open to one of the Upper Freight Holds. Max glanced in - no one was there, but this room had a window to the outside.

And Max gasped in surprise.

Off to the side of the ship was

AT FIRST, HE THOUGHT IT WAS A WEIRD SQUARE SPACE-STATION, PERHAPS SOMETHING NEW THAT'D BEEN BUILT IN THE BETA QUADRANT. BUT THEN IT MOVED.

something he'd never seen before. At first, he thought it was a weird square space-station, perhaps something new that'd been built in the Beta Quadrant. But then it moved.

"It's a ship," Tori gasped, and Max quickly got her away from the window. He didn't have a clue what the strange square block was, but he had realized that it was what his ship was firing at.

"C'mon."

Another hit, and the Lalo really rocked this time. With a cry, Tori toppled and went sprawling along the floor, which was now at a sharp angle. Furious with himself for losing her grip, Max grabbed her arm and she yelped at the force. But Max didn't have time to apologize.

He closed his eyes, working out the quickest route to Deck 6, counting off bulkheads and Jeffries Tubes in his mind. It didn't have to be the 'right' route, the 'approved' one, it just had to be the quickest, and, if someone yelled at him later, well tough.

The Lalo shook again, but this was no explosion nearby.

"Tractor beam," Max yelled.

Then he realized something. That weakness in Decks 8 and 9. If the attackers could be made to use their tractor beam there, the hull would buckle, yes, but then the tractor beam would very soon have nothing to grip. It was their only hope - and only Max had realized this.

He needed a comms unit. He needed to contact Dad. No, he needed to contact the Bridge.

But power was out, so even if he could find one, it would be useless.

As Max turned to tell Tori his plan, he felt a massive wave of heat wash over him, and he was on his knees. Tori was crying now. "Where's everyone else?"

But Max was worried about the explosion.

Another plasma fire, this one just behind them, had consumed the entire corridor.

The flames were rolling towards them.

They had to move.

"Run, Tori, run!"

He ran, almost dragging Tori behind him, this time determined not to let go of her.

And then it struck him. Tori was

right, they simply hadn't seen anyone else. Was everyone on this deck... dead?

Dad!

Dad couldn't be …

No, of course not. Dad would be fine. And he'd listen to Max and find a way to maneuver the ship, so the tractor beam would hit the right point on Decks 8 and 9.

Max was right, there was a stairwell here. They needed to go down and he got Tori to go first. They just needed to get down to De-

When Max woke up, he had no idea how much time had passed, he could only guess that the ship had been hit again and something had blown up, knocking him sideways into a corridor.

Where was Tori? She wasn't there with him. Had she kept going towards Deck 6? Towards Dad. He hoped so. Max tried to get his bearings, work out where he was. Shouldn't be difficult, he told himself. You're the genius, you're the expert in all things *Lalo*. He staggered up and realized quickly that he was indeed on Deck 9, three decks away from Dad. He spent a few more minutes searching for Tori, but no, she had

kept going. Good for her, it was the right thing to do.

As Max walked forwards, towards where he knew another stairwell down would be, he could hear people. Not shouting, not yelling, just murmuring. He couldn't work out what they were saying. So he moved towards the sounds.

And stopped.

These weren't people. These were... something else. Dressed in black, with grey skin and weird tubes and metal and... there was one whose left arm was actually some kind of metallic claw-like device. One of them turned towards where Max was now hiding, just at the edge of the corridor. A thin laser beam of light strafed the wall and after it vanished, Max gave a careful glance round. The light was coming from an eye-piece, over one of the invader's eyes.

Max looked closer and gasped. These weren't just the black-clad

invaders. There were Starfleet crew and officers, as well! Chief Engineer P'uress was there, similar implants attached to her leg and face. How'd they managed to do this so quickly? Max guesstimated it had been maybe thirty minutes since the first warning, since Dad had gone to his station. Whoever these people... these creatures were, they moved fast. What were they doing to the crew?

Max stepped back.

And a hand grabbed his shoulder. He knew it was Dad. He could recognize that grip anywhere. And yes there, on the hand, was the ring. The wedding band with Celtic inscriptions.

"Dad!" Max cried.

And stopped.

Dad was staring at him. One shoulder was covered in silver machinery. Was he hurt? Had the doctor patched him up? Then, Max realized Dad's right eye was covered in a patch that was clicking and whirring.

And three thin black tubes were linking his neck to the back of his head.

"Dad?"

"You understand this Starfleet ship," said Dad. But it didn't sound like Dad.

And a thin back tube emerged from Dad's finger and stabbed into the back of Max's hand. Max tied to pull away, but his father's grip was too tight, and Max started to feel his legs give way.

"Dad..." he wanted to scream, but his mouth didn't work.

"Resistance is futile," said the voice coming from Dad's mouth. But it wasn't his Dad's. It wasn't a voice Max had ever heard before. And it seemed to echo inside his head.

"Your knowledge of Starfleet ship design will be added to our own."

The last thing Max saw was the wedding band on his dad's finger. And he knew he'd never find out if Mom still wore hers... ⬩

Scramble

STORY: GREG COX
ILLUSTRATION: LOUIE DE MARTINIS

San Francisco, 1941 (or a reasonable facsimile thereof)

"This is your last warning, gumshoe. Drop this case if you know what's good for you."

Private detective Dixon Hill, as played by Captain Jean-Luc Picard, wasn't about to be intimidated by a low-level hoodlum like Mickey Giza, and certainly not in his own office. Sporting a trench coat and fedora, he stepped protectively in front of his latest client, a blackmailed heiress currently embodied by Deanna Troi. "I'll be the judge of that, Giza."

"Don't be so sure." The two-bit weasel pulled a pistol on Picard. "This is between 'Slugger' Kagan and the little lady here. Keep your nose out of it."

Picard weighed his options. Could he disarm Giza or should he keep him talking instead? Before he could decide what Hill would do, a shot rang out, blasting the pistol from Giza's grip. Spinning around, Picard was startled to see that Troi was no longer portraying Laurel Dupree, glamorous socialite, but rather was decked out, holographically, as a Wild West gunfighter, complete with a cowboy hat, a gunbelt slung across her hips, and a smoking six-shooter in her hand.

"Vamoose, you no-good varmit, before I fill your mangy carcass full of lead."

"Deanna?" Picard said, breaking character.

"Call me Durango," she said with a grin.

Picard recognized the character from a western holodeck program Troi enjoyed on occasion. But what was "Durango" doing in a Dixon Hill mystery?

"Computer, freeze program."

The hard-boiled scenario paused, turning Giza as stiff as a storefront mannequin, as Picard regarded Troi's incongruous outfit quizzically. "An explanation, Counselor?"

"I'm as puzzled as you are, Captain." She blew out the smoke wisping from her firearm. "Not that I didn't take full advantage of this unexpected twist."

"More like a malfunction. It would appear that a computer glitch is causing one recreational holo-program to bleed into another. No doubt a result of our recent mishap."

The *Enterprise* was undergoing shipwide maintenance after a close call with a dark matter nebula resulted in minor damage to the ship and its systems. Nothing too critical, but requiring attention from La Forge and his engineering teams. Inspecting the holodeck was obviously a low priority, unless . . .

"Computer, verify safety protocols are still in place."

"*Confirmed*," a disembodied female voice confirmed.

Picard nodded. "Merely an aggravation then, not a crisis." Scowling, he observed that the view from Hill's office now included the Eiffel Tower. "A pity this case will have to resume another day. I'm afraid I owe you a rain check, as it were."

"Why not continue?" She suggested.

He didn't understand. "But the program has been compromised, so there's no point in carrying on until it's been fixed."

"Because?" She prompted.

He gestured at the window, at her cowgirl getup. "These anachronisms are spoiling the integrity of the story."

"So? With respect, Captain, why not just relax and give it a go anyway? Who knows, it might be fun. You just need to put your preconceptions aside and open your mind to new possibilities."

"You're beginning to sound uncomfortably like Q," Picard grumbled.

Then again, with the *Enterprise* cruising at impulse during the repairs, they weren't arriving anywhere soon. And he *had* invited Troi to join him on this holo-adventure during their downtime, so he was reluctant to disappoint her, nor to appear too inflexible.

"Very well, although I fully intended to stay in character – if possible." He raised his voice.

"Computer, resume program."

Giza picked up where he'd left off, making tracks while spewing threats. "This ain't over, Hill! Just wait until Slugger hears about this. You'll be sorry, and Annie Oakley here, too!"

He slammed the door on his way out, leaving Picard to review the narrative so far. "Slugger" Kagan was a notorious mobster who was blackmailing Laurel over some highly embarrassing letters he'd come into possession of. She'd just hired Hill to get the letters back when Giza had barged in – and Durango had replaced Laurel.

> "A PITY THIS CASE WILL HAVE TO RESUME ANOTHER DAY. I'M AFRAID I OWE YOU A RAIN CHECK, AS IT WERE."

"So what's our next move, pardner?" She drawled.

Picard was pondering that when, abruptly, a gunshot went off outside in the hall and they heard Giza cry out. Sharing a glance, Picard and Troi dashed out of Hill's office to investigate, only to find themselves in an elegant dining car, rattling along a vintage railway line.

The Orient Express?

"All right, detective," a bristling Tellarite wearing a monocle and a tuxedo challenged Picard. "You've got us all gathered here. Why don't you tell us whodunnit?"

Mickey Giza was nowhere to be seen, dead or alive. Instead Picard found himself, along with Troi, in a different variety of detective story, where the assembled suspects provided more evidence that the holodeck's glitches were escalating, given that the group consisted of a green Orion nun, a human standup comic of some notoriety, an Andorian flapper from the Roaring Twenties, one of the three Musketeers, and . . . Sigmund Freud?

"A fascinating conundrum. Perhaps we should consider the unconscious urges behind the murder." Freud puffed on a cigar. "Then again, sometimes a red herring is only a red herring."

Picard paused the program again. "This is absurd!"

"Or delightful," Troi countered, "depending on your attitude."

"Look here, one of the pleasures of genre is familiarity: you enter a Dixon Hill mystery, you know what to expect, within certain established parameters, and those parameters are what define the work. Without boundaries, a haiku is no different than a sonnet." He gestured at the ridiculous mishmash surrounding them. "Musketeers and cowboys do not belong in a hard-boiled detective story."

"Perhaps, but sometimes blurring those boundaries, or even throwing them out entirely, can be rewarding, if only just to let your imagination and creativity run free. Like mixing chocolate with peanut butter, or staging a modern-dress version of *Aida* set on Romulus."

"I did once see a production of *Macbeth* set during the Eugenics Wars," he conceded, somewhat grudgingly, "that provided a fresh way to look at the classic tragedy." He sighed before giving in. "I suppose we can see out this . . . scramble . . . a bit longer."

* * *

"Blast it, Hill," the posh Tellarite demanded as the program resumed, "don't keep us waiting. Who is the killer?"

"Yeah," the flapper's antennae twitched impatiently. "And what's

with Calamity Jane here?"

Not surprisingly, Picard felt as though he'd missed a few chapters of this particular mystery. "Er, 'Slugger' Moran?"

"Who wants to know?"

Kagan stormed into the dining car, clearly looking for trouble. At this point, Picard was only slightly surprised to discover that the 1940s mobster was now a Klingon in a pin-

"I'VE HAD ENOUGH OF YOU, HILL! TIME TO TEACH YOU A LESSON YOU'LL NEVER FORGET..."

striped suit, sporting brass knuckles instead of a *bat'leth*. Trailing behind him was Giza, now unaccountably a Ferengi, complete with a bandaged lobe from when he was presumably shot before. Kagan snarled at Picard.

"I've got a score to settle with you, Hill!"

"Hold on!" The Tellarite said. "I thought the killer was one of us?"

"It is!" The chartreuse nun pointed at Freud. "I can keep silent no longer. It was the professor in the baggage coach with an umbrella!"

"*Ach!*" Freud exclaimed. "That was not my superego, only a monster from my id!" He seized the flapper and held an entirely non-period hypospray to her throat. "Permit me to take you hostage, my dear."

"Unhand her, miscreant!" The musketeer sprang to his feet and drew his rapier, accidentally impaling the comic, who chose precisely that moment to dash in front of him. Picard wasn't sure if that constituted good comic timing or the reverse.

"Take my life, please!" The comedian crashed into a table, sending plates and dishes flying. "And don't forget to tip your waiter . . ."

Pandemonium erupted. Snorting furiously, the Tellarite tackled the musketeer, obstructing Kagan, who shoved the nun aside in an effort to get to Picard, even as the flapper elbowed Freud in the gut and flipped him over her shoulder toward Troi, aka Durango, who knocked him

out with the butt of her six-shooter, then dived into the all-out brawl, throwing punches and whooping it up, while Picard stomped on the fallen hypospray to keep it from falling into the wrong hands, as well as on general principle.

"Saints preserve us!" The nun crossed herself, only to fritz, stutter, and morph into a certain Goddess of Empathy, clad in a flowing Grecian robe, who just happened to be a dead ringer for Deanna Troi. "Please, dear souls, turn away from violence and seek peace and harmony instead."

Rolling her eyes, the real Troi snatched a custard pie from a dessert caddy and smashed it into her doppelganger's beatific face.

"Was that strictly necessary?" Picard asked.

"Absolutely."

Kagan ducked a flying bottle of champagne, flung by the flapper, then stumbled over the comic's skewered body. The bottle shattered behind him, spraying him with foaming spirits.

"For Kahless's sake! This was a new suit!" He shook a fist at Picard as he fled the car. "Another time, Hill!"

Picard was tempted to let him

go, but knew that Dixon Hill would stay on the case, no matter what. He shoved his way through the melee. "We're not through here, Kagan!"

"Not so fast, gumshoe!" Giza plucked the rapier from the comic's corpse and tried to stab Picard in the back, but Troi lassoed him just time, yanking him backwards.

"Go," she urged Picard. "I've got this!"

Taking her word for it, he took off after Kagan, exiting the dining car and chasing his quarry through:

The bridge of James Kirk's original *U.S.S. Enterprise* (no A, B, C, or D).

The rocking deck of a 19th-century sailing ship.

A romantic moonlit beach.

And, finally, as the environment kept shifting around them, the blistering heat of Vulcan's Forge, where Kagan finally turned to make a stand.

"I've had enough of you, Hill! Time to teach you a lesson you'll never forget..."

"My thoughts exactly." Picard reached inside his trench coat for his gun, but pulled out a badminton

racket instead – just as the holodeck gifted Kagan with a Klingon *painstik*. *Merde.*

Picard again considered shutting down the program, but resolved to stay on the case, even if it meant a trip to sickbay afterwards.

But perhaps there was a way to turn these glitches to his advantage? "Make up your mind," he challenged Kagan. "Are you a human criminal – or a Klingon warrior? Who ever heard of a lowlife mobster with honor?"

"I . . . that is . . . *Qapla'*?"

The questions flummoxed the hybrid character. Conflicting subroutines froze Kagan long enough for Picard to wrench the *painstik* from Kagan's grasp. Energy crackled furiously as he gave the mobster a taste of his own medicine, dropping him onto the hot, barren soil.

"You messed with the wrong gumshoe," Picard said. "There's a reason I get twenty bucks a day, plus expenses."

A dust cloud on the horizon turned into a damp pea soup fog as a horse-drawn hansom cab rolled out of Victorian London. Troi exited the carriage, thanking the coachman for

the lift.

"Just watch yourself, young miss," he replied "and stay off the moors. I know what I saw, and those were the footprints of an enormous *targ*!"

Meanwhile, Picard had one last bit of business to attend to. Frisking Kagan's unconscious form, he retrieved the incriminating letters from Kagan's vest pocket. He handed them to over to Troi, who set them ablaze with a struck match. "Thanks, pardner."

"Case closed," Picard said.

* * *

"All right, Counselor," he conceded, after shutting the holodeck down for maintenance. "That exercise did turn out to be somewhat exhilarating. Perhaps there *is* something to be said for taking liberties with any given setting or story . . . if only just for novelty's sake. Occasionally."

"That's the spirit, Captain," she said. "Who knows? Maybe next time I can be Dixon Hill and you can be Durango." ⌞

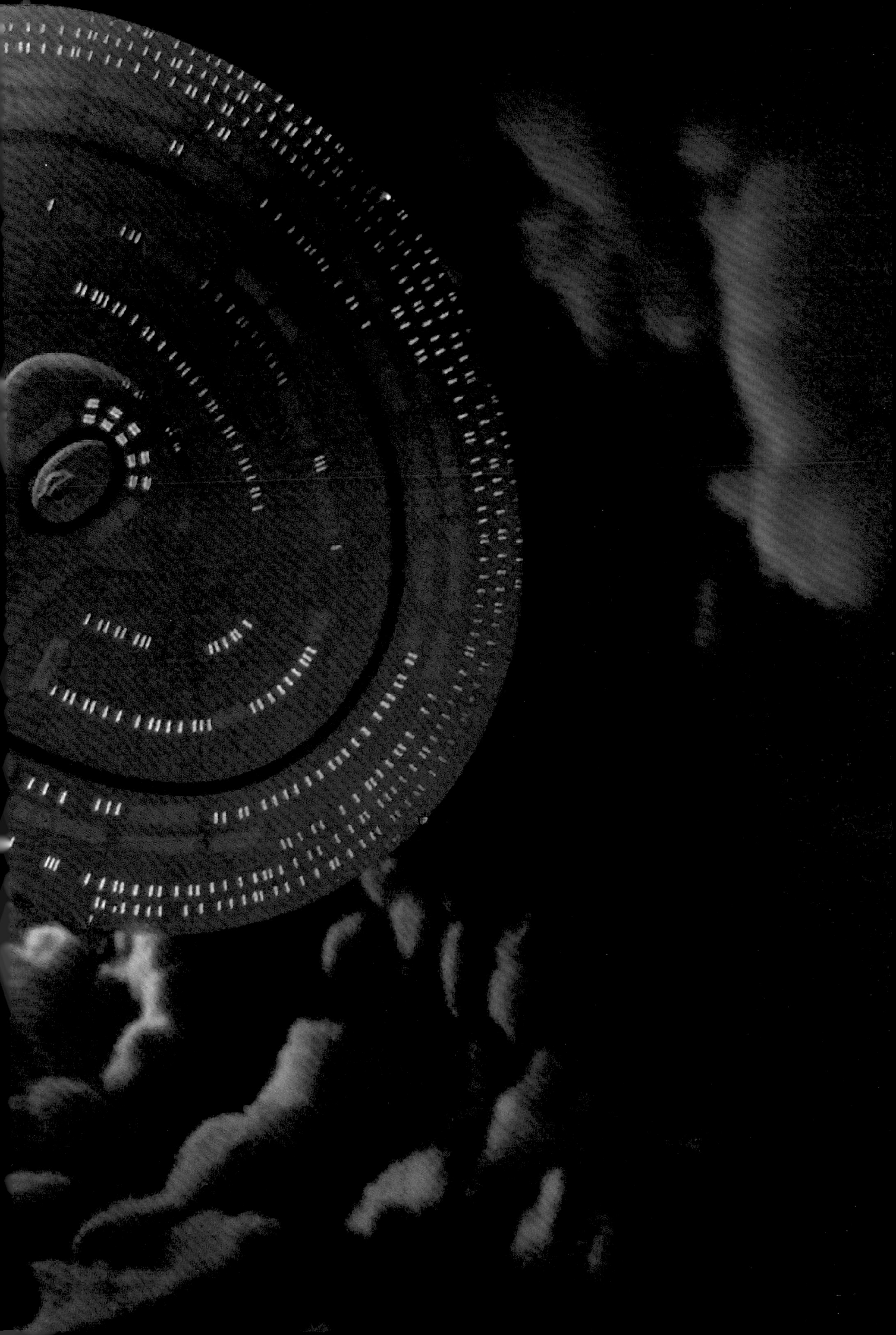

The Mission

STORY: JAMES SWALLOW
ILLUSTRATION: LOUIE DE MARTINIS

*(Author's note: this story takes place in 2374, during the Dominion War, prior to the
events of the* **Star Trek: Deep Space Nine** *episode "Inquisition")*

ection 31 Hyperchannel XCF-221-1
(Encrypted)
      **Sender Identity: Sloan, Luther /
Recipient Identity: [REDACTED]**

*Here's everything I've managed to scrape together
about the disappearance of the operative we dispatched
to Deep Space 9. It's sketchy at best, fragments of
personal logs and security recordings – and that in itself
is troubling. But I'll let you review the data and draw
your own conclusions rather than burden you with
mine.*

*   I will preface this with just one statement: the
following material proves this approach was flawed, as
I warned you it would be. Let* me *handle things with
Sisko and his people from here.*

*   I have a potential asset in place... I just need time
to bring him into the circle.*

**Personal log, Mission Day 5: Operative Sierra
(Encrypted)**

    I've found accommodation in one of the outer
rings of this iron-clad monstrosity, in a zone used
by transient workers and Bajoran nationals up from
the homeworld. My cover identity is as an Akaali
migrant looking for employment as a maintenance
technician, and so far there have been no challenges
to its veracity. The genetic alteration of my human
characteristics are solid, enough to fool any cursory
tricorder scans. I can pass for at least three months
before additional doses of bio-masker are required.
The other residents show little interest in me, which
is ideal. Most of their discussions I overhear at the
replimat revolve around how uncomfortable the
station is; I concur. Cardassian architecture cares
little for creature comforts.

    My mission parameters remain as assigned.
Objective Alpha: conduct surveillance on Captain
Benjamin Sisko and his command staff. Objective
Beta: Utilize my skills to penetrate Deep Space 9's
computer network and embed digital implants for
Section 31's remote monitoring. I'll make my first
attempt to place the sensors during tomorrow's
morning shift.

**< Security Feed G-2345, DS9 Officer's Quarters
Level >**

< Time index: 37:47:32 >

Playback display: corridor interior.

*   Subject #1 (humanoid, species: Akaali) enters
visual. Pauses in shadow behind support pillar.
Removes device (identified as covert microsensor bead)
from satchel. Proceeds to affix device to upper section
of pillar.*

*   SOUND: doorway opening.*

*   Subject #1 reacts with alarm. Conceals device.*

    SUBJECT #2: *[terse]* Can I help you with
something?

*   Subject #2 (humanoid, species: Changeling) enters
visual. Body language and vocal tones suggest suspicion
and annoyance.*

    SUBJECT #1: *[submissive]* No, I'm... I'm fine.
[pause] You're... Constable Odo, is that right? The
shapeshifter?

    SUBJECT #2: Very observant. What gave it
away?

    SUBJECT #1: I, uh...

    SUBJECT #2: That was a rhetorical question.
What are you doing here? I know your face, you're
one of the new workers from out-system.

    SUBJECT #1: I'm Lonia. Lonia Kefal. From

Akaali.

SUBJECT #2: Well, if you're seeking employment, I suggest you start by looking for it at the labor office on the Promenade, not down by the senior officer's quarters.

SUBJECT #1: Apologies! This is a very big station, and the corridors all look alike! I must have gotten turned around.

SUBJECT #2: Then allow me to escort you back to where you need to be. Consider it a courtesy of Station Security.

Subject #2's intimidating presence compels Subject #1 to depart with haste.

Personal log, Mission Day 7: Operative Sierra (Encrypted)

What was the likelihood that the Changeling would be there at the worst possible time? I cannot be certain, but I believe he was exiting quarters belonging to Kira Nerys, the station's second-in-command. Perhaps they are engaged in a non-work relationship? File that observation for later consideration.

Did my cover raise a concern when I boarded DS9? I must assume Odo will be suspicious of me for the interim. I have already placed

microsensors near Sisko's and Dax's quarters, they will have to suffice.

For now, I'll concentrate on Objective Beta – computer network infiltration. This will be a painstaking process... I must work my way into the station's mainframe slowly and carefully, or else I risk detection by internal monitor software.

< Security Feed K-0372, DS9 Promenade Level, Replimat >
< Time index: 78:33:11 >

Playback display: dining area.

Subject #1 (humanoid, species: Akaali) is seated, reading a PADD, drinking a mug of liquid (soup: Plomeek).

Subject #2 (humanoid, species: Cardassian) approaches. Offers Subject #1 an isolinear rod.

SUBJECT #2: [brightly] Good afternoon! May I give you this?

SUBJECT #1: [wary] What is it?

SUBJECT #2: A voucher! For a discount. I find it an ideal way to

stimulate business. [pause] I like to offer one to selected new arrivals...

SUBJECT #1: [reading] "Clothiers and Tailoring"... "Garak's Clothiers"?

SUBJECT #2: [bowing] The very same! Has my reputation for service reached all the way to Akaali Prime?

SUBJECT #1: I'm not sure I really need a tailor...

Subject #2 studies Subject #1's tunic in great detail.

SUBJECT #2: Are you quite certain of that? When one is looking for gainful employment, the first impression at an interview can make or break the application. And if you don't mind me saying, your outfit... could use some refinement. [pause] Unless, of course, you have some other work to occupy you?

Subject #1 returns the isolinear rod, and leaves the table.

SUBJECT #1: Thank you, but no. If you'll excuse me, I have an appointment elsewhere.

"DID MY COVER RAISE A CONCERN WHEN I BOARDED DS9? I MUST ASSUME ODO WILL BE SUSPICIOUS OF ME FOR THE INTERIM..."

Personal log, Mission Day 11: Operative Sierra (Encrypted)

The Cardassian spoke to me today. I cannot be certain if the interaction was random, or if he is aware I am not what I appear to be. Nevertheless, I took the opportunity to cover the route back to my quarters and once there, to run a full-spectrum surveillance scan. I found no evidence of tracking devices on my person or in my room, but my pre-mission briefing on the Cardassian was very clear – avoid Elim Garak at all costs! Even if this so-called tailor is no longer an agent of the Obsidian Order, I cannot interact with him.

I will lay low for a few days and take my meals at the refectory on the lower tiers. Hopefully, we will not cross paths again.

Personal log, Mission Day 20: Operative Sierra (Encrypted)

In five days, Bajoran Standard,

I am due to report in to Section 31 via subspace burst-communique, but I am seriously considering an emergency transmission.

Last night, during the station's Delta Shift, I took the opportunity to check the microsensors I planted near Sisko and Dax's quarters. They have been neutralized. The work is extremely subtle. On the surface, they appear to be recording the targets' comings and goings, but the data is flawed. It is *faked!* Someone has reprogrammed the sensors to give false readings, to conceal Sisko and Dax's actual movements...

It's a clever strategy. I almost didn't notice.

But who aboard the station has the skill to do such a thing? The Cardassian? The doctor with the genetic enhancements, or perhaps the Trill herself? Or is it possible I am not the only covert operative embedded on Deep Space 9?

I need to consider my next move.

Personal log, Mission Day 20, supplemental: Operative Sierra (Encrypted)

I have been unable to sleep. I keep dreaming that I am being followed.

The situation with the microsensors preys on my mind, so I decided to check on the progress of my network intrusion program...

...I have found something very alarming. Far more serious than the co-opted sensors.

My program has now wormed its way into the core of the station's main computer, and if all was proceeding to plan, it should have automatically deployed a software payload there – in theory, giving Section 31 a hidden back-door into Deep Space 9's command and control systems, should it be required.

But something was already there.

Understand that this station's mainframe is a retrofitted mess of overlapping operating systems – the original programs from when it was constructed by the Cardassian occupation forces, then a layer of Federation and Starfleet software atop that. It is ugly and complex, and full of places for rogue files to hide!

In these dead digital spaces I found... I can only classify them as *scraps* of code, the remains of old programs that were purged from the system. But I could identify them, even so, as a body might be identified from a faint remnant trace of DNA.

The first scrap is part of a *shaipouin*; that's a Romulan word meaning 'false door'. This is a code-tool used by Tal Shiar intrusion specialists. The second was a remnant of a brute-force data-wiper with a Klingon signature, likely a data bomb left behind by Imperial Intelligence on *Qo'noS* before it was deleted. And there was a third...

Timecodes indicate the last

"I HAVE ALLOWED MYSELF TO BECOME CAUGHT UP IN THIS MYSTERY... BUT I CAN'T LET IT GO."

program was erased recently, perhaps only days before I arrived. It has the unique structure I've only seen in one other place. The hijacker programs utilized by the Orion Syndicate.

Romulan. Klingon. Orion. They've all sent agents here before me. *But what happened to them?*

< Security Feed Q-8255, DS9 Promenade Level, Quark's Bar >
< Time index: 44:18:82 >
Playback display: bar area.
Subject #1 (humanoid, species: Akaali) converses with Subject #2 (humanoid, species: Ferengi).

SUBJECT #2: An Orion, you say? To be honest, I don't see many of them in my establishment. The Syndicate and the Ferengi Alliance tend to stay out of each other's way, if you know what I mean.

SUBJECT #1: He was on the station for a few months. Surely someone remembers?

SUBJECT #2: [quietly] I'm not one to judge, if Orions are to your... taste. But I can offer alternatives, if

you'd like. My holosuites are the best in the sector.

SUBJECT #1: [firmly] That's not what I mean! One day, he vanished, and I need to know what he knew—!

Subject #3 (male humanoid, species: Changeling) enters visual.

SUBJECT #3: If someone went missing on my station, I would be aware of it.

SUBJECT #2: [dour] Constable, always such a delight to see you.

SUBJECT #3: I'm hearing that our Akaali friend here has been asking about an Orion shuttle pilot who left the station some time ago. I can assure you, his departure was logged with Ops.

SUBJECT #1: [aside] Logs can be falsified.

SUBJECT #3: That's a very serious accusation. Can you back it up with any evidence? Or perhaps you'd like to explain exactly *what* your interest is in this Orion pilot?

Personal log, Mission Day 25:
Operative Sierra (Encrypted)

I have allowed myself to become caught up in this mystery... But I can't let it go.

I have to find out where these other agents went. The Tal Shiar was masquerading as a travelling scholar from Vulcan, the Klingon agent was a crewman transferred off a freighter, and the Orion...

Despite what the Changeling claims, I've found evidence to the contrary. The pilot was last seen heading to the station's lower core. The old ore processor is down there, left over from the days of the Cardassian Occupation.

I am supposed to report in today. I am going to delay that until I have investigated.

I must find answers!

< Security Feed Z-9992, DS9 Lower Core Level, Ore Processor #3 >
< Time index: 25:84:00 >
Playback display: ore chamber.
Subject #1 (humanoid, species: Akaali) enters. Activates tricorder, scans interior of processor through an open

maintenance hatch.

SUBJECT #1: [muttering] There's a DNA trace in there… Can't read it clearly. [sighs] Need to get closer…

Subject #1 climbs into ore chamber, approaches interior wall with tricorder.

SOUND: tricorder chiming.

SUBJECT #1: Positive reading! Traces of Orion bio-matter, but very faint… They've been disrupted by an energy pulse…

Beyond Subject #1's point of view, Subject #2 (humanoid, species: undetermined) enters the chamber in shadow and moves to a control console.

SUBJECT #1: Is someone out there? [panicked] What's going on? Stop what you are doing-!

Subject #2 reactivates the ore processor, closing the hatch. Subject #1 is now sealed inside.

SOUND: banging noises and muffled shouting from inside the chamber.

Subject #2 engages the processor's energy pulse field. A yellow glow fills the visual.

Section 31 Hyperchannel XCF-221-1 (Encrypted)
Sender Identity: [REDACTED] / Recipient Identity: Sloan, Luther

Luther: I must reluctantly concur with your evaluation. It appears that Operative Sierra was not the best choice for this assignment. They allowed themselves to become focused on minutiae to the detriment of the mission, and it would seem they paid for that with their life. Analysis indicates this was likely a trap, deliberately set to snare any covert operative sent to Deep Space 9. From the data recovered, we can surmise that a similar fate was met by the Tal Shiar's agent, the Klingon spy from Imperial Intelligence and the Orion.

We must tread carefully with DS9 in our future dealings with Sisko and his crew. The captain himself may be reluctant to cross certain ethical lines, but it appears that at least one member of his inner circle has no issue with taking active – and quite ruthless - measures.

Efforts to recruit your potential asset are hereby officially approved.

< Security Feed K-0372, DS9 Promenade Level, Replimat >
< Time index: 66:15:06 >

Playback display: dining area.

Subject #1 (humanoid, species: Terran) is seated, drinking a mug of liquid (coffee: raktajino).

Subject #2 (humanoid, species: Cardassian) approaches.

SUBJECT #2: My dear Julian, please accept my most humble apologies for my lateness.

SUBJECT #1: Hello Garak. I was starting to think I'd been stood up…

SUBJECT #2: Never! I value our conversations too highly to miss one.

SUBJECT #1: I hope I didn't drag you away from something important.

SUBJECT #2: [smiles] I'm ashamed to say I was working on a thorny problem and I simply…lost track of time.

SUBJECT #1: Anything I could help with?

SUBJECT #2: Nothing you need concern yourself about, Doctor. I was just…*cleaning house.*

'Things Can Only Get Better'

STORY: UNA MCCORMACK
ILLUSTRATION: LOUIE DE MARTINIS

T his mission to retrieve the Breen ship had pushed them all to their limits and, in some cases, Kira suspected, well beyond. They'd barely started when Damar learned about the death of his wife and son, and he ended up shooting his friend, Rusot. Odo was sick – no, Odo was *dying*, Kira must face up to that, must admit that – and now he lay helplessly on a bed in the infirmary, hoping that somehow Julian would perform some miracle. As for Kira herself – there was nowhere she wanted to be less than on board this flyer heading toward Cardassian space. She wanted to be sitting with Odo, holding his beloved hand, giving whatever consolation she could. How desperately she wanted to see him. How bitterly she regretted all the time they had wasted…

"Commander," said Garak, from the seat beside her, "I wonder if I might trouble you to check on the engine's power emissions, please?"

Kira pulled herself into focus and ran the check. She glanced sideways at Garak, at the helm. Of all of them who had been on that mission, only Garak seemed unperturbed by everything that had happened – but then how would you know, with Garak?

"All good," said Kira.

"Thank you," said Garak. "I'd be grateful, Commander Kira, if you could stop your mind from wandering. We're very close to the border now, and the likelihood of Jem'Hadar patrols increases by the moment."

Well, *that* was testier than usual. Kira said, "You've got my full attention."

"Thank you," said Garak. "I can run this blockade alone, but I'd rather not."

Maybe he hadn't much enjoyed the mission either. Still, she didn't need a lecture from him. "I said you've got my full attention."

"Good. In that case, could you run a check on the weaponry readout? I'm still not satisfied they'll pass any serious sensor sweep."

They were using a civilian flyer to get back into Cardassian space, but one armed to the teeth with a judicious selection of Starfleet photon torpedoes. Garak had rigged the sensor readings so that they would show up as more or less defenceless, but if there were any discrepancies, it wasn't likely that the Jem'Hadar patrols operating in this area would give them a chance to explain themselves. Kira had carried out this check half a dozen times already, but if it kept him happy…

"And the long-range scanners when you're done," said Garak.

"Anything else while I'm at it?" said Kira.

"I'll let you know," said Garak.

"Is Damar still in the back?"

"Since he isn't here, you can assume so."

"Maybe we could do with his help," said Kira.

"I'd rather he rested before returning to the base," said Garak. "It's not every day you get news that your family's been murdered."

Where had *that* come from? "I didn't mean –"

"Oh, I'm absolutely sure you didn't."

This was getting ridiculous. Kira leaned back from the console and turned to face him. "Garak, if there's something you want to say to me – say it."

"I'm simply trying to ensure we don't get killed before we enter Cardassian space. I've waited such a long time to get home. I'd prefer not to die at the border."

"I'm not planning on getting any of us killed."

"Good." Yellow lights flashed across the display in front of them. Ships, not too distant. "Jem'Hadar patrol, most likely," said Garak.

"I'm on it," said Kira, and began to chart a course correction to get them away if necessary. Easy enough – if your mind was on the job.

"Not that you'd mind adding a couple more spoonheads to your overall count, I suppose," said Garak.

"Excuse me?"

"A former Cardassian head of state… An ex-Obsidian Order agent?" Garak was nodding. "Damar and I must both pose very tempting targets."

"Well, you *hadn't*," said Kira, "until you mentioned it."

"Forgive my skepticism. Killing Cardassians is practically second nature, surely?"

"Oh, you've got some nerve!"

"Have I."

"Come off it, Garak! Your hands are at least as bloody as mine. And I don't even mean Bajorans. The Obsidian Order must have killed hundreds of thousands of Cardassian civilians—"

"Oh, that wasn't my department." Garak gave a careless wave of the hand, as if to brush off the accusation.

"Data entry, that was my specialty. I have an abiding love for statistics –"

"Keeping count, huh? So how many Cardassians have met their fate at your hands?"

His face was a mask. "I never relished it."

"Meaning that I did?"

"Commander," he said, giving her a very steady look, "only you can answer that for sure."

Kira took a deep breath. If he'd been trying to get a rise out of her, he'd succeeded. A mistake on her part. She wasn't sure what purpose these mind games served for Garak, but she knew better than to participate.

"Could you take the helm, please?" said Garak. His tone was quieter. Perhaps he too was regretting the savage turn this conversation had taken. "I'm going to get something to drink."

"*Sure.*"

"IT'S NOT EVERY DAY YOU GET NEWS THAT YOUR FAMILY'S BEEN MURDERED."

Garak went off to the replicator. Kira ran her hands through her hair and shook herself. She needed to get a grip. They *all* needed to get a grip. They weren't going to make it through this alive if they kept tearing at each other. The Dominion was the enemy. Attacking each other only did the Founders' work for them. Still, Garak was right about one thing. Fighting Cardassians – *killing* Cardassians – was the habit of a lifetime, and one you didn't easily break.

There was a sudden crackle of static on the comm. A signal? Kira worked on boosting it and was soon able to pick out a repeated pattern, one that she knew well. A Cardassian distress call. She'd been the cause of more than a few of those during her life.

"*Civilian freighter… under attack… urgent assistance…*"

"That doesn't sound good," she muttered. She charted the ship's position. Close to their current course. Maybe if they got a little closer, she could find out more…

"What's going on? Why have we picked up speed?"

Kira glanced over her shoulder. Garak was standing behind her, his eyes narrow, holding a mug of rokassa juice. Typical. That stuff *stank*.

"Distress signal," she said. "Call for aid." She opened the comm channel again.

"Civilian freighter... under attack... urgent assistance..."

Garak took his seat again. "Do we know who they are?"

"There's a lot of interference on that channel," she said.

"Let me try," said Garak. He worked quickly, competently (he was always competent, you had to give him that). "Here we are," he said.

Suddenly the message was coming through, loud and clear. A young man's voice, very scared.

"This is the civilian freighter Pelosa. *We are travelling with seventy-eight refugees from Kelvas IV. We are under attack... We need urgent assistance... Repeat, this is civilian freighter* Pelosa..."

"Do we know who's attacking them?" said Kira.

"One moment..." said Garak, checking sensor readings. "I'm getting... two Jem'Hadar ships."

"...refugees from Kelvas IV. Please – if there's anyone out there, hurry! We don't have much time..."

"They're outside Cardassian space," said Kira, suddenly.

"So?"

"That means they're our responsibility."

"I'm not sure I agree... Commander, *what* are you doing?"

Kira was busy with the controls. "Plotting an intercept course. We should help."

"I don't think that's wise—"

"They need our help."

Suddenly, a grey hand was on hers, stopping her from operating the controls. A Cardassian hand, on hers. "If we intervene," said Garak, softly, "our cover will be blown. This isn't our responsibility. We already have our mission."

"Garak," said Kira, looking straight into his bright blue eyes.

"Yes, commander?"

"Take your hand off mine or I'll break both your wrists."

They stared at each other. In the background, the message played on. *Help us... Help us...* Kira watched Garak's lips curve into a smile. She thought, *I'd relish that – and he knows how much I would...*

Garak released his grip. "I'd rather you didn't," he said. "My needlework would be never the same again. But you do know, don't you, that we need to leave well alone."

"No," said Kira, shaking her head.

"If we intervene," said Garak, "we will have to reveal ourselves, and that might put the resistance at risk. We have to maintain cover and continue our mission."

"There might be something we can do."

Garak sighed and sat back. "I can't stop you," he said. "Not without incurring an unacceptable degree of damage to my person. But you know I'm right."

Through the comm, they heard an explosion. People screaming. The voice, when it spoke again, was barely in control. *"Please! Please, someone, help us…"*

Those voices… So easy to picture what it must be like on board. How many Bajorans, trying to get to safety,

"HOW MANY CARDASSIANS HAVE MET THEIR FATE AT YOUR HANDS?"

had suffered a fate like this? Ordinary people, kids many of them, sent off by parents, trying to escape horrors, risking themselves on rickety little freighters, only to be shot out of the sky by warships, Cardassian warships…

"We'll move a little closer," said Kira. "Take some readings of those two Jem'Hadar ships. See if they've taken any damage. Maybe we can pick them off…" She looked

at Garak, sitting back in his chair, sipping his appalling drink. "Are you going to help me fly this ship?"

"You're on your own with this. Unless you want to threaten me again. Break a wrist, an arm, a leg? I won't be much help, though, incapacitated."

"Forget it," she said. "I can do this myself."

"Be my guest."

Kira started to plot a course to intercept the Jem'Hadar ships. Did they have enough fire power? Suddenly, she was beset with doubts. What if they didn't? What if she crashed into the middle of this fight only for them to be blown to pieces? What a waste, what a pointless waste…

Get a grip, Nerys. They're in Federation space. This is the right thing to do…

The flyer was turning. She calculated four-and-a-half minutes before she would be able to open fire. She opened her mouth to ask Garak to report on the status of the nearest Jem'Hadar ship, but when she

saw his face, she gave up getting any help from him. She tried to take the readings herself, all the while keeping an eye on their new course and speed and trying not to feel too much of those cries for help…

"Why are you bothering? Why are you putting yourself through this?" said Garak. He sounded genuinely curious. "There's nothing to be done without blowing our cover. And we can't blow our cover."

"The real question," said Kira, "is why you aren't bothering. Listen to them! They're helpless, desperate! There must be something we can do –"

"You know as well as I do that there's always collateral damage in war—"

"Collateral *damage?*"

"Our mission," said Garak, "is far more important that a handful of refugees. What do the Vulcans say? 'The needs of the many –'"

"They're civilians!" said Kira.

"*Cardassian* civilians. They know their duty. And besides – what's a few more dead spoonheads in the great scheme of things?"

"It's not their *fault*!"

Garak's expression changed. Was that… was that *compassion*? "You know, commander, you and I…" He swallowed. "We've been living a long time now with the Federation. Learned to do things the Starfleet way. But we both know some wars can't be won like that."

There has to be another way… There has to be a better *way…*

"The Federation changes people," said Garak. "It's time we changed back."

Through the comm, they heard Jem'Hadar pressing their attack. Heard explosions. Systems going critical. A minute, maybe less… She could open fire, save lives, do the right thing, be the *hero*… But that wasn't why she had been sent on this mission, was it? They hadn't sent the liaison officer, the diplomat, the first officer. They'd sent the fighter. The killer.

"Kira," said Garak, gently. "Let it go."

Kira's hands hovered over the console. She breathed, in and out. Moved her hands away. "Reverse course," she said. "There's nothing we can do here."

Garak, leaning forward, quickly obeyed her instruction. Through the comm, the voice cried out, *"Please! Please help us!"*

There was another explosion. Some screaming. Then static. They were gone.

"We did the right thing," said Garak

"No we didn't," said Kira. "That wasn't right. But it was —"

"Necessary," said Garak. "Yes. I know."

The flyer moved on. Kira's head was buzzing. Maybe she should get some sleep too. After a couple of minutes, Garak sighed, and said, "I'm pleased to report we have crossed the border into Cardassian space."

"Hey," said Kira. "You made it home after all."

"Yes," said Garak. He didn't sound particularly happy. Just tired. "Yes, I did."

Movement behind them. They both turned – quickly, guiltily, partners in crime. Damar was there, rubbing sleep from his eyes, looking very disheveled for a hero.

"I thought I felt the ship move," he said, and yawned. "Something the matter?"

"Don't worry, legate," said Garak. "Commander Kira has everything under control."

There was still static coming through the comm. Kira reached out and cut it, dead.

Frontier Medicine

STORY: MICHAEL CARROLL

ILLUSTRATION: LOUIE DE MARTINIS

entle laughter and the clinking of cocktail glasses reached Julian Bashir even before the turbolift's doors opened.

He stepped out into the cruiser's opulent reception room to be greeted by wide smiles and firm handshakes from people who seemed far too eager to be his friend, which did little to quench his imposter syndrome: his graduation from Starfleet Medical Academy was still eight days away and yet here he was, being treated to a luxury cruise to the Ferenginar system by the Onotark Corporation. They did this every year hoping to recruit the Academy's best and brightest as medical researchers.

After ten minutes of uncomfortable small-talk with an Andorian woman who laughed a lot but never smiled, Bashir spotted a familiar face and politely excused himself.

Standing with his hands casually clasped behind his back and peering down at the long buffet table, Stosk glanced up as Bashir approached. "Julian."

Bashir surveyed the wealth of food on offer. "I must say, I could get used to travelling first-class." He turned back towards the other partygoers, all dressed in their finest and looking immaculate. Keeping his voice low, he said, "But they are laying it on a little *thick*, wouldn't you say?"

Stosk nodded. "Indeed. When they interviewed me I was clear that my loyalties could not be bought, yet they still invited me on this trip."

"They promised me a staff of eight, top-of-the-range equipment, and an unlimited budget. You?"

"Comparable. I would be permitted to spend twenty per cent of my time on projects of my own choosing."

Bashir smiled. "Hah! Well, now, I can see why that would be very tempting for you! Unless you've abandoned the search for a better treatment for Purggraf's?"

"I have not." Stosk abruptly turned his attention back to the buffet table, and nodded at one tureen in particular. "*This* one has more the appearance of a terrarium than a dish. There are live creatures within."

"Probably beetles," Bashir said, backing away a little. "The Ferengi do have a fondness for crunchy arthropods."

"I would suggest that almost all arthropods, as they possess an exoskeleton, would be considered crunchy by most standards."

"True."

Vulcans didn't give away much, but Bashir knew he'd hit a nerve. Early in their first year in the academy, Stosk had come to Bashir for advice: "Julian, I have chosen to study Purggraf's Toxaemia. It is a—"

"Don't tell me, I *know* this one," Bashir had said, eyes closed as he dredged up the memory. "Parasitic infection, extremely rare. One hundred percent fatal in humanoids if the correct treatment is not administered at the correct time. After the initial infection it becomes dormant and undetectable. It's so similar to our own microbes that it passes through even the most stringent teleporter filters. At some point between eight and eleven years after infection, the parasite begins to release a venom that will kill the host within four days if not treated. Correct?"

Stosk nodded.

"And the treatment itself… Blood-platelet filtering to purge the venom, then tightly-focused bursts of x-rays to destroy the parasite itself. And that's the tricky part, isn't it? Finding and killing a single lightning-fast microbe-sized beastie with a beam a hundredth the diameter of a human hair."

"Again, correct. I wish to discover a faster, more effective treatment."

They had pondered on the problem on-and-off over the following eight months, and made little progress, but that wasn't the point. It was the shared puzzle that they'd enjoyed, the distraction from countless lessons about much more common ailments.

Now, the best part of a decade later, it occurred to Bashir for the first time that perhaps Stosk had not chosen to study the rare condition on a whim… but this wasn't the time to ask about it.

They quickly moved past the bowl of squirming, sauce-drenched beetles in search of more palatable dishes.

"Tree-mould salad," Bashir said. "That looks safe enough. Can I tempt you?" He reached out his hand and as his fingers touched the serving spoon it juddered out of the way. "What…?"

The floor trembled and the dishes on the buffet table rattled.

"That's… worrying," Bashir said. "We're travelling at warp *seven*…"

Stosk finished the thought. "There should not be turbulence."

A familiar high-pitched note behind him – a transporter. Bashir spun around in time to see a circle of armor-clad figures materialize in the center of the stateroom, each one facing outwards, large guns in their hands.

A tall, broad-shouldered human male in full body-armor fired his gun into the ceiling. "Everyone face-down on the floor! Hands where we can see them!"

The partygoers quickly got down on the floor, and Bashir did the same, but a crew member – a young Ferengi – had remained standing, his arms outstretched, hands open and empty. "Please," he addressed the circle of intruders. "Let's all remain calm. If it's *money* –"

The large man stepped away from the circle, glowering at the Ferengi. "Ears like that, and you still got a problem hearing? Or maybe it's a problem *listening*?"

"I… I don't under–"

He swung the butt of his gun in a smooth, practiced arc that intersected with the Ferengi's head, knocking him to the floor.

Bashir instinctively began to move towards the Ferengi, but a firm voice beside him said, "*No.* Remain in place, Julian."

He looked up to see Stosk calmly walking towards the intruders. "Mister Irons. So the time has come?"

The man nodded, and tapped the comm-badge on his collar. "He's here. Beam her in."

Behind him, the armed intruders each took a few steps forward, widening the circle, as a teleportation glow appeared at its center.

Bashir recognized the machine: an old med-pod. Seventy years out of date, at least, but they were still in common use on the fringe worlds. At the heart of the pod, strapped to a vertical table and hooked into it with dozens of tubes and cables, a middle-aged human woman scowled at Irons. "Get this done."

"Make progress," Irons said to Stosk, "and make it fast." He scowled around the room once more. "Any heroics, any noise, anything I don't like, you all die. Do *not* test me on this."

As Stosk began to examine the med-pod's readouts, Bashir couldn't help doing the same. There was something familiar about the

"EVERYONE FACE-DOWN ON THE FLOOR! HANDS WHERE WE CAN SEE THEM!"

configuration of the tubes and attachments. *Filtering her blood… And that's a modified X-ray emitter bolted to the side. Elevated heartrate, slightly low pressure, temperature two point six degrees above normal…*

He watched as Stosk tweaked the pod's controls… and knew now what was happening. The patient was suffering from Purggraf's Toxaemia.

Stosk is working with them. He's part of their group. Must have enrolled in Starfleet Medical just to study the disease… and all this time they've been waiting for that tiny window before death when the condition is treatable.

Now, the Vulcan was running a medical tricorder along the woman's outstretched left arm.

"Well?" Irons barked. "What's taking so long?"

"This is a delicate procedure, Mister Irons," Stosk replied. "It cannot be rushed. The parasite tends to lodge in the extremities but… pinpointing its location could still take several hours, if not days."

"Days?" the woman said. "Stosk, I don't *have* days. If word gets out that I'm sick my up-line will dismantle my operations and hand the pieces to my rivals. You do *not* want to be on my bad side if that happens."

Bashir took a deep breath. "I can help."

Irons pulled a large, laser-edged knife from his belt. "You can *die.*"

Stosk said, "No! I… Bashir is a more accomplished physician than I. We… *need* him."

The woman narrowed her eyes as she gave Bashir a slight smile. "Julian Subatoi Bashir. Yes, I know your name. Word is you're the cream of this year's crop. Let him up, Irons."

Bashir pushed himself to his feet, clenched his fists to stop his hands from trembling as he approached the med-pod. He raised the woman's arm and pulled back her sleeve. "Distended veins…" He gently reached out towards her right eye, pulled up the lid. "Look up. Now down… Jaundicing, myokymia. and a touch of strabismus… The venom is already taking hold." He turned to Irons. "I need a *general-purpose* tricorder, not a medical one. And remove your left glove: put it on the patient's left arm."

The big man smirked. "You don't give me orders, boy. I'm the one—"

"You'll do as I say if you want your boss to live. Unless you've already made contingency plans with *another* faction of the Orion Syndicate?"

"No one questions my loyalty! You—"

"Just do it!" the woman snapped. "Get him the tricorder—and the glove!" She turned back to Bashir.

"You're as insightful as Stosk's reports suggest, Bashir. My name is Seph Magdiel, and, yes, I do have connections with the Syndicate. I'm impressed that… you were able to deduce that."

"Your people boarded a ship travelling at warp speed by magnetically locking their armored suits to the hull before beaming themselves in. That's one of the Syndicate's signature moves."

Magdiel smiled. "I'd offer you a *job*, Bashir, but I know you… you wouldn't…" Her voice faded as her head dropped to one side.

"She's out… Tricorder – now!"

Irons handed him a general tricorder, and he flipped it open and held it over Magdiel's heart. "Temperature's climbing, respiration becoming labored… Irons, the glove. Quick as you can. Stosk, disable the blood-filtering."

The Vulcan was rapidly typing on a datapad linked to the med-pod. "Julian, that would permit the venom to build and greatly shorten the patient's life-expectancy."

"I *am* aware of that. Now do as I say, Stosk!"

A large hand grabbed Bashir's arm, spun him around. Irons' laser-knife was inches away from his face.

"ANY HEROICS, ANY NOISE, ANYTHING I DON'T LIKE, YOU ALL DIE. DO NOT TEST ME ON THIS."

"You think you can get out of this by *killing* her?"

Bashir dry-swallowed, but refused to look away. "I took an oath to preserve *all* life, Mister Irons. Trust me, this is her best option."

Irons stepped back. "You'll save her or I swear I'll obliterate every last –"

Bashir had already stopped listening. "Stosk, on my mark, hit her with a one-second X-ray burst, lowest setting, full-body." He flipped open the tricorder and held it over Magdiel's heart.

As he maneuvered the X-ray emitter into position, Stosk said, "Julian, the parasite cannot be detected by an ordinary tricorder. It –"

"The parasite is hard to kill because it's *fast*. It runs from the X-rays straight through the heart to the first safe place it can find." Bashir peered at the general tricorder's display. "We can't detect the parasite itself, but we can detect its *venom*. The venom contains minute traces

of necrodioxide. Because that's so rare, a medical tricorder detecting it will double-check and *triple-check* in case of an erroneous reading. That process takes a few seconds, but that's long enough to be fatal. A general tricorder will report *instantly* when it detects the necrodioxide." He turned to Irons. "You understand what you have to do?"

"I… yes. She is *not* gonna like this."

"Not my top concern at the moment." Bashir looked from Irons to Stosk, and back. "No hesitation… Take hold of her wrist, and get ready. Stosk… Do it!"

It took less than a second. The Vulcan activated the X-ray emitter, bathing the patient's body in a brief white glow—

- Bashir saw the tricorder's readout blink, and yelled, "Now!" –

- and Irons lashed out with his laser-knife.

Seph Magdiel's left forearm slipped out of Irons' armored glove and thumped heavily to the floor, the wound already cauterized by the white-hot knife.

Bashir stared at the medical tricorder. "Come on… come on…" He stepped back, unable to hide his grin. "Venom levels have stabilized – we *got* it. Stosk, restart the blood-filtering to purge the remaining venom."

He picked up the severed arm and handed it to Irons. "A souvenir."

Magdiel recovered consciousness as Stosk was disconnecting her from the Med-Pod. "You… you cut off my arm!"

"It was the only option," Bashir explained. "The glove shielded your arm from the X-rays, gave the parasite a safe place to hide."

The woman looked down at the stump. "I guess I've had worse." She turned to Irons. "We're done here."

"We should plunder," Irons said. "Ship like this is worth millions –"

"No. We take nothing." Magdiel leaned on Bashir's shoulder as she stepped away from the med-pod. "I owe you for saving my life, Doctor. And I'm repaying that favor right now by allowing everyone to live."

Bashir nodded. "That's… generous."

She smiled. "You'll be an exceptional physician, Julian Bashir. But *this*…" With her remaining arm she gestured to take in their lavish surroundings. "This is not for you. You should go where people need you most. On those pampered Federation worlds there's little you can do that others can't. But out there, on the *edges*, where supplies are low, and needs are desperate… There you can make a *real* difference."

As he beamed out with the intruders, Stosk raised his hand in a Vulcan salute. "Thank you, my friend."

Bashir didn't notice. He was already tending to the young Ferengi crew-member. ⬩

By Special Request...

STORY: JOHN PEEL
ILLUSTRATION: LOUIE DE MARTINIS

hief Miles O'Brien slowly relaxed as he sipped his drink in Vic's Place on the holodeck. It had been a rough day, as – once again! – Cardassian technology had broken down on Deep Space 9, this time taking down the alpha cascade circuitry on the main transmission network. It had taken O'Brien and his crew six hours to root out the problem and arrange a working bypass that would last them until Federation replacement parts could be shipped in. He really felt that he deserved this downtime and the cold beer before heading back to his quarters. Keiko wasn't off-duty for another two hours, and he didn't feel like being entirely alone just yet.

Vic's Place was the obvious solution. It was one of the most popular holodeck programs, and one shared by plenty of people. Some of the tables were occupied by holograms, but quite a number had real customers. Vic Fontaine was a personable manager/singer who specialized in Golden Oldies from seven worlds, and who employed a couple of Bajoran singers to spell him as needed. It was sometimes easy to forget that Vic was, in fact, a hologram himself.

Speak of the devil… O'Brien saw the singer heading his way, with Julian Bashir in tow. The two were talking in an animated fashion, and Miles adjusted his slouch as he realized that, whatever the two were discussing, he was likely to be called on to join in. He liked the young and rather brash doctor, but Bashir could get quite passionate at times – and generally at times when O'Brien simply wanted to relax…

"Miles," Bashir asked, before Vic could begin, "a question: How alive would you say holograms are?"

Not at all what he had been expecting. He blinked and gathered his thoughts as Bashir and Vic slipped into seats at the table. In the background, a pianist was playing lazy improvisations. "Well," O'Brien said finally, "two thoughts occur to me there. First – you're a doctor, so you're undoubtedly more qualified to decide on life than I am. And, second – well, second, it depends on how you want to define *life*. It's a bit tricky sometimes."

"See, that's my point," Bashir commented. "I mean, I'd agree with you that *normally* I'd be able to say whether somebody was alive or dead –"

"Oh, good," O'Brien muttered.

"But – holograms?" The doctor shook his head. "That's kind of tricky ground. You're an engineer, though, so it seems to me that it falls into your area of expertise, not mine."

O'Brien sighed. "Why not ask the *real* expert?" He gestured at Vic. "Straight from the horse's mouth, so to speak?"

"But Vic's *programmed* to believe he's alive," Bashir protested. "Uh – no offense, Vic," he added, a little embarrassed.

The singer grinned amiably. "None taken – after all, *you're* programmed to believe you're alive, too."

"Not programmed," Bashir insisted. "Born. You were *made*."

"Ah, well, you're getting on difficult ground there, Julian" O'Brien felt compelled to say. "I mean, Commander Data was *made*, too – but he's as alive as anyone I know. Starfleet even granted him human rights."

"That's my point," the doctor said, eagerly. "Data's an android, but one who is sufficiently complex and self-aware so he undoubtedly meets the criteria of being alive. Now – are holograms sufficiently complex and self-aware, too? I don't mean *legally*, but *practically*."

"The birds, the bees and the microchips," Vic murmured.

"Well, there was an instance on the *Enterprise* where a hologram certainly seemed to come to life," O'Brien admitted. "Moriarty…

But that was a unique case." He glanced around the room. "Most of the holograms in here have minimal awareness – just sufficient to perform their roles as background actors, so to speak."

"But if I went up to…" Bashir glanced around and then pointed to a Bajoran couple at a distant table. "Those two, say. They're just background. But if I went over and spoke to them, they'd respond."

"Yes," the chief agreed. "The computer would augment their minimal programming and temporarily give them a little personality. But it would vanish again once you left."

"But what about starring holograms – like Vic here?"

"Well, he's imbued with a greater degree of personality, of course."

"Thank you," the singer said, wryly.

"But how much greater?" Bashir asked.

"Very much greater," O'Brien said. "A completely different level. He has to interact and to improvise constantly. He also has to remember what he's said in previous interactions. He has to sing – and, more importantly, he has to be able to inject personality into his songs, otherwise they'd simply be dull and flat. So he has to *seem* alive. But whether he *is* alive… I'm not sure I can say. Sorry, Vic."

"Quite alright, my friend," the singer replied. "It's what I've been wondering myself. As you said, I was programmed to feel as though I were alive – but is it possible that I have grown beyond my programming?"

"How do you mean?" O'Brien's beer was forgotten now; he had become intrigued.

"You said that the computer augments programming to holograms as it is needed," Vic argued. "Could it have added enough extra to me to have caused me somehow to have

"IF HE IS JUST A HOLOGRAM PROGRAMMED TO REACT BY A COMPUTER, *HOW* COULD HE POSSIBLY WISH FOR ANYTHING?"

skipped over from non-life to life? After all, this Data you mentioned was a cybernetic creature. At some point, he was merely components, but when they were assembled, he appears to have become alive."

Bashir couldn't completely hide his smile. "And, if you think about it, isn't that true even of living *organic* beings? One point, not-life; at another, life?"

O'Brien found himself growing more interested in the issue. "But all of the holograms created on the holodeck are formed and constructed by the station's computer," he pointed out. "And *that* is not alive… Could something non-living create true life? After all, Data was created by Dr. Noonian Singh, and *he* was alive."

"And we – who are living – created the computer that created Vic," Bashir responded.

"It's an interesting thought," the chief admitted. "And I honestly don't think I'm qualified to pass judgement on it." He looked earnestly at Vic. "Honestly, I'd like it if you *were* alive, but I can't see any way we could really prove it."

"I think I may have," Bashir admitted, softly.

"Really?" O'Brien was fascinated.

"How?"

"Because he said something to me a short while ago that I don't believe he could have done if he wasn't alive."

O'Brien grinned. "This I have to hear. What was it?"

The doctor turned to the singer. "Tell him what you told me," he ordered.

Vic spread his hands. "I merely said that I had a wish."

O'Brien was puzzled. "That's it?"

"That's it," Vic agreed.

The chief turned to Bashir. "Julian, you've lost me completely. How does that prove he's alive?"

"Miles, *think!*" the doctor said eagerly. "He's *wishing* for something he doesn't have. Something he *wants*. If he is just a hologram programmed to react by a computer, *how* could he possibly wish for anything? All he would know, all he *could* know, is what he has. But to wish – ah, you have to be human to desire more than you already have. Or Bajoran," he added hastily, "or something else that's alive."

O'Brien had to admit that the doctor seemed to have something there. To desire something else meant that Vic wasn't entirely satisfied with his life as it was… and how could something that was merely a computer

program – no matter how sophisticated – be dissatisfied? The ramifications of this possibility were intriguing – and startling. For one thing, if Vic was indeed alive… did they have any right to turn off his program? It wasn't like killing him – maybe more like putting him to sleep – but did they have any right to force him to sleep?

This was going to be a headache.

"So," Bashir asked, "are you going to help me to help him?"

"What?" O'Brien jerked his attention back. "Help him? To do what?"

Bashir sighed. "Honestly, Miles, there are times I wonder about you. Help him to get his wish, of course."

What am I now? The chief wondered. *A genii?* "You'd better tell me what it is," he said.

So Vic did.

* * *

Naturally, it wasn't a simple wish. But it did prove to be doable. Eventually. It took a week to organize, but once O'Brien's enthusiasm was engaged, he wasn't going to give up on it despite the obstacles in the way. Thankfully, he had a very understanding wife, and once Keiko had been informed

she joined in. She understood how obsessive he could become when he was working on a project, and she supported him and listened to all of his thoughts.

The next person to convince was Captain Sisko.

"A duet?" he asked, baffled. "Vic wants to sing a duet?" He frowned. "Why bring this to me? Surely you can just program him another singer?"

"It's not that simple," O'Brien had to explain. "It's not just *any* duet – it's a *specific* partner he wants to sing with."

Sisko snorted. "Well, if having a wish *does* somehow make him human, having a difficult wish makes him *very* human. Very well, why do you need my help?"

"Because Federation law makes it illegal to make a hologram of a living person without their authorization. I'm sure you can see how such a duplicate could be abused."

Of course Sisko could, in any number of ways. "So you need to contact this person, then, and get their permission? I understand – but why do you need my help?"

"Because of who it is." O'Brien told him who was wanted.

"I'll do what I can," the captain promised.

* * *

There was a real air of expectation in Vic's Place. It had been a chore to arrange the schedules so that the main crew could all be present for this very special event. They were all there, gathered about the stage, and chattering excitedly amongst themselves. O'Brien and Keiko were seated with Bashir and Jadzia Dax. Captain Sisko had Kira and Odo at his table. Even Quark had managed to tear himself away from his bar for the evening, despite the lure of latinum to be made. O'Brien was surprised to see that even the perennial barfly Morn had deserted Quark's for once to silently nurse a drink at a more distant table. Well, it was a very special performance on a very special night. Nobody wanted to miss it.

There was a round of applause as the band came out and took their places. They started tuning up.

"Can't they get on with it?" Keiko muttered impatiently.

O'Brien patted her hand. "They want everything to be perfect," he reminded her. "It will be worth the wait."

"I know, I know…"

He couldn't blame her. They had worked so hard to arrange this, and the time seemed to have slowed to the pace of a lethargic amoeba. Bashir started tapping his fingers until Dax put her hand firmly over his to stop

him. O'Brien glanced around, and saw that even Sisko was starting to fidget. Where was Vic? Building anticipation was one thing, but he might be overdoing it…

And then the lights went down, and a single spotlight illuminated the piano. A spontaneous burst of applause accompanied Vic as he moved down the stage to stand beside the instrument. He was grinning widely as he bent his head in acknowledgement.

"Ladies, gentlemen and gentlebeings," he said. He was trying to stay calm, but there was a detectable tinge of excitement in his voice. "Welcome to a very special night at Vic's place, and to a very special guest star. I'd like to thank everyone who helped to make this possible – but I suspect there might be a riot if I did. So, instead, let me introduce, by special request and for one time only…"

The spotlight moved away from him to the curtain at the rear of the stage, and there was a huge round of applause and cheers as he finished:

"Nyota Uhura!"

And the legend stepped into the bright light, her microphone at the ready, as she began.

"Beyond Antares…"

In memory of Nichelle Nichols, the Great Songbird of the Galaxy

The Victim

STORY: JOHN PEEL
ILLUSTRATION: ANDY WALKER

'I'm afraid I'm here to kill you.'

Vedek Shawah inclined her head slightly and regarded her late-night visitor with interest. 'You're here to kill me,' she murmured, 'and *you're* afraid?' She stood aside and waved her hand to invite him in. Then she carefully closed the door behind him.

'You know what I mean,' the Cardassian said, a little peevishly.

She examined him carefully. 'I know you,' she decided. 'You pretend to be a tailor... Garak, isn't it?'

'I *am* a tailor,' he protested. 'The best one on Terok Nor.' He looked rather proud. 'My father was better, but he taught me well.'

She snorted in amusement. 'Tailor *and* assassin,' she said. 'You're something of an over-achiever, aren't you? Well, hadn't you better get on with it?'

'Get on with it?' He echoed.

'Killing me.'

Garak blinked rapidly and peered at her. 'Aren't you afraid?' He asked. 'Aren't you going to try and talk me out of it?'

Shawah sighed. 'You're new at this, aren't you?'

'Well, yes,' the tailor admitted. 'I've never actually...' His voice trailed off.

'Killed anyone?' She said, gently.

'Yes. That.'

'Then why are you starting now?' She asked.

He sighed. 'Orders. I'm to kill you and make it look like a botched robbery.'

She surprised him by actually laughing at that. 'Nobody will actually believe that,' she pointed out. 'I am not a wealthy person. I have few possessions. I need no more.'

'It's not really a matter of what people *believe*,' he replied. 'It's what they can *prove*, isn't it?'

She snorted. 'That's what your superiors *believe?*'
She asked, ironically.

'Yes, well, they're only my superiors in rank. Not necessarily in intelligence.' He couldn't keep the bitterness from his voice.

'You don't like these orders,' she said gently.

'No,' he admitted. He shuffled uncomfortably. 'Don't get me wrong – I'm as patriotic as the next Cardassian.'

'Just not as homicidal?'

'I'm a spy,' he said, rather proudly. 'I *like* being a spy.'

She eyed him perceptively. 'It feeds your ego,' she decided. 'It makes you feel superior to everyone around you.'

Garak scowled at her. 'You're making fun of me. It's not a clever idea to make fun of your executioner.'

'Please forgive me,' Shawah said. 'I'm a vedek. Do you know what that means?'

He shrugged. 'You're some sort of religious personality. The Bajorans feel a need for your kind of people.'

'But you, of course, don't?'

'We Cardassians take responsibility for our own lives. We don't pass along blame or praise to some sort of mythical beings.'

'Well, we'll let that pass for now,' she replied. 'But, as a religious leader, one of my tasks is to try and show people how to better themselves.' She spread her hands apart. 'I can't help doing that, even with an alien tailor, spy, and assassin. The Prophets have charged me with a mission, and I must follow the path that they lay before me.'

'At the moment,' he pointed out, 'your path is to die.'

She smiled, somewhat sadly. '*Everyone's* path is to die. It's merely a matter of recognizing and accepting this.' She studied him again. 'And it appears that my path is about to come to its end. So be it: I accept what the Prophets have appointed for me.'

'These Prophets of yours aren't doing this,' he said. '*I* am.'

'But you aren't,' she informed him. 'You're trying to squirm out of your path. You've been sent to kill me, and yet – well, here you are, talking and not killing me.'

He stared at her. 'You *want* me to kill you?'

'Of course not,' she said, crossly. "Not in the way you mean. I may be an old woman, but that doesn't mean I'm tired of living. But I *am* committed to following the will of the Prophets. And it appears that they have decided that I am to die. In that case, I am ready to do their will – with you, of course, acting as their instrument.'

'I am *not* their instrument,' he snapped crossly.

'No? Well, let us say that you believe that you're the instrument of your Cardassian masters. It shouldn't

"EVERYONE'S PATH IS TO DIE. IT'S MERELY A MATTER OF RECOGNIZING AND ACCEPTING THIS."

matter all that much to you that I believe something quite different.'

He winced, as if she had struck him a blow. 'Well, I can see why they want you out of the way: you're quite mouthy.'

She laughed. 'Yes,' she agreed. 'I not only point out *your* failings, but mine as well. I do tend to talk a lot, don't I? And it upsets your people, because I refuse to repeat the platitudes that the Cardassians wish me to pass along. They want me out of their way in the hopes that they will be able to use me as an example to make other vedeks toe their line.' She snorted again. 'It won't work, you know. Any self-respecting vedek listens to the Prophets and not the invading forces.'

'Perhaps my superiors would allow you to live if you were to change your message?' Garak suggested.

'Now you're reaching,' she replied. 'Perhaps they might – but I would not change what I say. I must obey the Prophets, as you must obey your masters.' She settled herself in her favorite seat. 'Come along, tailor – do what you are here for.'

Again, he hesitated.

'You are on dangerous ground, my friend,' Shawah told him. 'You *must* fulfill your mission. It is the only way ahead for both of us.'

He started to pace in front of her, back and forth, nervously and irritably. 'I am a spy,' he growled.

'I thought you were a tailor?' She .said, slightly mockingly. She really ought to control that tongue of hers!

'Yes, I *am* a tailor,' he agreed. 'And a good one. And I'm a good spy. I enjoy being both of these things.'

'But you're a terrible assassin,' Shawah concluded.

'Because I *don't* enjoy that.' He stared at her. 'I don't think you should die simply because you talk too much.'

'But your superiors do,' she pointed out. 'They don't like my message of peaceful resistance to your people.'

'They don't like *anyone* who disagrees with them,' Garak muttered.

And *now* she understood. 'You don't agree with them,' she said softly. 'Do they know that? Or do they simply *suspect* it?'

'I'm not a fool,' the tailor replied. 'I can keep my mouth shut.'

Shawah chuckled. 'Except, it would seem, with me.'

'You're supposed to die,' he said. 'Which would then remove

that problem.'

'If you can bring yourself to do it.' She shook her head. 'Which, at this moment, doesn't appear to be too likely.'

'I told you,' he said with some heat. 'I'm a spy, not an assassin.'

'And *that's* the problem, isn't it?' He scowled. 'What do you mean?'

She snorted. 'Oh, come on, Garak! Cardassia has plenty of assassins, hasn't it? Too many, in fact. So – ask yourself *why* they send a tailor to do an assassin's task.' He stared at her bleakly, but she could see that he was starting to understand her point. 'I think this task is perhaps more to do with ascertaining your degree of commitment to the Cardassian cause as it is about silencing a Bajoran dissenting voice.'

He was silent. She could see that he was in the grip of conflicting emotions. She wished she understood the invaders' emotions better, so

"I ACCEPT THAT THIS IS A JOURNEY THAT I MUST TAKE..."

that she might know whether this was a good or bad time to urge him onwards. Would it be better to stay silent and allow him to think this through? If it was a Bajoran she faced, she'd know, but she had never been able to fully grasp the Cardassian mentality.

Naturally, he reached the wrong conclusion. 'I won't do it!' he growled. He pulled a phaser from his tunic and laid it on the table between them. 'I have more self-worth than that. I refuse to sink to the level of a mere killer for them.'

'And what good do you imagine that decision will do either of us?' she demanded.

He blinked. 'What do you mean?' It seemed that he understood her no better than she understood him.

'You've been sent to kill me, Garak,' she said gently. 'If you go back and tell them that you refuse to do it, do you think that your handlers will simply say "Oh, that's alright then; we'll let her live"?'

He sighed. 'That's not very likely, is it?'

'It's not at all likely,' she growled. 'They will simply send a true assassin to finish the mission, and I'll be dead anyway.' She looked at him with compassion. 'And what do you think will happen to you if you refuse to carry out your orders? Will they pat you on the back and commend you for your courage?'

'No,' he admitted sadly. 'I suspect that I would perish even more quickly than you. But I won't have degraded myself. I won't have killed an innocent person.'

"And what a comfort that would be to both of us,' she mocked. 'Besides, I'm *not* at innocent person. I am guilty of exactly what upsets them – I speak of resistance. And resistance is never futile.'

'So… What are you saying?' He demanded. 'That I should pick up…' He stared at the phaser. '*That*, and use it on you?'

'Yes.'

'You *want* to die?' He cried.

'I think it's become obvious to both of us that this is the path that the Prophets have set before me,' she said gently. 'And because I trust the Prophets, I accept that this is a journey I *must* take.' She smiled bleakly. 'In a sense, then, you could say that I want to die, because that is the path before me.'

'That's insane,' he replied bitterly. 'These Prophets of yours don't exist! You can't be serious about following them.'

"Garak.' She rested a hand gently on his arm. 'We all have to believe in something greater than ourselves. For me, it is the Prophets. For you? Ah, there you must choose. I know my path, and I accept it with gladness. And, yes, a little fear. Death is the unknown, isn't it? It is only on the far side of death that I will discover whether or not my faith is true. But what is *your* path going to be? Where will it lead you? You have three ways to travel. First, you can stand firm and refuse your orders. That way leads to your death as well as my own, but it is death with dignity, should you choose it. And that is not a bad way. But is it the best? And in the second and third ways, you fulfill your mission and kill me.

'In the second way, you accept the way your superiors have chosen for you. You become their tool, as I have been the tool of the Prophets. You cast aside your beliefs and assume theirs.

'And then there is the third way. You do what you must to survive. But you keep your own counsel, your own beliefs, and you work for *them*, and not for the orders you are given. You resist. You walk your own way.

'I cannot choose for you – only you can select your path. But select it you must.'

He stared at her bleakly. 'You wish me to take that third way.'

She shook her head. 'What I wish is not relevant. It is what *you* wish that is at stake.' She picked up the phaser, and placed it into his pliant hand. He gripped it almost without willing to. 'My way is clear – I go to the Prophets. Be assured, I am not a victim. But you?' She smiled gently. 'Which of us is the true victim here?'

She closed her hand over his and pressed.

The phaser discharged.

You Can't Buy Fate

STORY: KEITH R.A. DECANDIDO
ILLUSTRATION: ANDY WALKER

tation log, Colonel Kira Nerys, Deep Space 9, Stardate 53018.4

We've been contacted by the Orrelhod Confederacy, a small nation from the Gamma Quadrant. I've sent Counselor Dax and Lieutenant Nog through the wormhole to make first contact.

As the Runabout *Sungari* emerged from the wormhole, Lieutenant (j.g.) Nog said, "Setting course 127 mark 4, speed warp five. We should rendezvous with the Orelhoddish ship in twenty minutes." Then he looked over at Dax, sitting in the copilot's seat. "By the way, Ezri, my uncle's holosuites should be fixed in time for your date tomorrow." At Dax's surprised glance, he added, "I saw the reservation list when I was scheduling the repair. Banerjee's set to work on it this afternoon."

Dax favored him with her bright and beautiful smile. "Thanks. Julian and I are gonna visit the Cliffs of Bole. And hey, it's good that you're delegating – it's the sign of a good chief of operations."

Nog hoped Dax couldn't see how happy seeing her approbation made him. "Uncle Quark doesn't think so. He doesn't want anyone but me working on his holosuites. But the colonel wanted me on this mission."

Tilting her head with amusement, Dax said, "Quark'll get over it. Besides, you don't want to miss the *first* first contact since the war ended, right?"

"Definitely not," Nog said with a small smile. Then, recalling a trip with Jake, Captain Sisko, and Uncle Quark five years earlier that went bad in a hurry, he added, "Let's hope it goes better than the first time I came through the wormhole in a runabout and made first contact…"

Putting an encouraging hand on Nog's, Dax said, "I'm sure it will."

Once again, Nog hoped Dax couldn't see how affected he was by the brief touch of her hand on his.

When Nog had first met Jadzia Dax, he was just a kid, and she was the Trill female who came to Uncle Quark's to play tongo. Jadzia was like family: a kind of eccentric, intimidatingly tall aunt.

When he had first met Ezri after Jadzia had been killed and the Dax symbiont implanted in the counselor, Nog was an adult, having been granted a battlefield commission during the Dominion War. When he was dealing with the trauma of losing his leg, Ezri had been there to help him.

Jake would have told him that it was just a crush, if Nog had possessed the courage to tell Jake (or, indeed, anyone) about how he felt about Ezri. But it didn't matter – she and Julian Bashir were a couple, and Nog couldn't compete with the genetically enhanced doctor.

A notification sounded on his console. "Entering the Beenserig system, dropping to impulse power."

Dax started running her hands over the console. "Sensors are picking up an Orelhoddish vessel fifty thousand kilometers off the starboard bow."

Nog started guiding the runabout toward the other vessel.

"They're hailing us," Dax said.

Looking to the comm screen on his left, Nog saw the face of an alien with golden skin, an oval-shaped head, cylindrical ear protrusions, four eyes, with a lengthy vertical slit that was apparently its mouth between the eyes. There was no evidence of a nose.

"To you fair travels we wish. Of the Orelhoddish Confederacy Shipmaster Rona I am called."

"I'm Lieutenant Nog of the United Federation of Planets. This is Counselor Dax." Before Nog could continue, he was distracted by an alarm. "What the –?"

"Wrong what is?"

The console was lighting up with several messages in red.

"We're having multiple systems failures!" Nog exclaimed.

Dax was also getting the alarms on her console. "Sensors are down. Navigation's down." The lights flickered out, plunging the runabout into darkness. "Main power's down."

"Emergency power is starting to fail, also," Nog said.

"Happening what is?"

"We don't know, but we may need to beam over to your ship."

"Expecting that we were. Ho –"

Then the screen went blank.

"Communications down," Dax said. "And the antimatter containment field is starting to fail also!"

"Computer," Nog said urgently, "emergency transport!"

"Unable to comply."

Before Nog could reach down to grab the emergency transport armbands, the warp core exploded…

When Nog regained consciousness, he had no idea who he was.

And then he realized it was worse than that.

He had *too many* ideas of who he was.

His mind was flooded with memories of things that never happened to him: holding a crying infant with small ears and spots down her sides, playing a keyboard, getting drunk with *Dahar* Master Kor, going on a hike with a woman he didn't recognize yet remembered as his sister, leaping through the air and twirling around three times before landing on his feet to applause, getting drunk with Captain Sisko, reading *Down the River Light* to his sick daughter, agonizing over a phase-coil inverter that wouldn't work right, getting drunk with Commander Worf, trying desperately to keep a broken-down shuttle from crashing, being shot by Captain Sisko, and *so much more…*

"What is happening!?" he cried out.

"Awake you are," said an Orelhoddish who was standing over him.

"What happened?" Nog asked. "Where am I?"

"On the vessel of Shipmaster Rona you are. Physician Krande I am. Dying your companion is."

Slowly, Nog sat up from the cot he was lying on. He felt something odd on his stomach and on his left leg, and then realized he was unclothed. Oddly, he was both mortified and unconcerned with his nudity.

There was a blue gel in a line across his stomach, and several other bits of similar gel on various body parts. His left leg now ended at the knee, the stump covered in the blue gel, and of his biosynthetic left leg he could find no sign.

He was in an oval-shaped room. Other cots were dotted about the space, only two of which were occupied: one with another Orelhoddish, and one with Dax, both of whom were also unclothed. Those two cots had holographic displays in an alien language hovering over them. Dax was also covered in many places

BEFORE NOG COULD REACH DOWN TO GRAB THE EMERGENCY TRANSPORT ARMBANDS, THE WARP CORE EXPLODED...

with the blue gel.

Physician Krande was standing next to Nog's cot. He had a thin torso, with four arms (two on either side of the center of the thoracic region) and four legs (protruding from the bottom of the torso).

Krande said, "As it was exploding off your vessel we transported you. Very long and hard our surgical team worked. Your anatomy we are unfamiliar with. Guess we had to."

"We need to contact DS9," Nog said.

"On their way your people are. In fifteen minutes they will arrive."

Even as his mind was crowded with dozens of unfamiliar memories, a more familiar one came to Nog now: the sensor reading he'd glanced before the *Sungari* exploded.

A section of the wall irised open, and Shipmaster Rona stepped through. "Awake that you are I am glad to see. In a vessel Colonel Kira is now approaching."

"You've got to contact her, tell

her to stay fifty thousand kilometers away from this ship!"

"Understand I do not."

"Your ship gives off Raejin Waves – it's an exotic radiation that I haven't seen in two hundred years. It's inimical to Federation technology." Even as he said it, Nog was boggled, as he realized he *had* encountered it two centuries ago during the Earth-Romulan War at a remote outpost.

When he was Tobin Dax.

The Orelhoddish had put the Dax symbiont in Nog. Given the presence of the blue gel on Dax's entire stomach area, she must have been wounded near the pouch, and Krande mistook the symbiont for one of Nog's organs.

Tobin never had figured out a way to counteract Raejin Waves, but something from Jadzia's time as a science officer clicked in Nog's head, and he realized that he knew a way he could modulate a Federation starship's shields to resist the waves!

But that needed to wait – Ezri

wouldn't last long without her symbiont, especially in a sickbay that didn't know a Trill from a Ferengi.

To Nog's relief, Rona wasted no more time with questions. "Colonel Kira, Shipmaster Rona. Fifty kilometers away keep your vessel please."

Kira's voice came over a speaker. *"Defiant to Rona. What's going on?"*

"Colonel, it's Lieutenant Nog." *"You're all right!"*

"Not really – long story, but Ezri and I both need medical attention *now*. But if the *Defiant* gets closer than fifty thousand kilometers, it'll blow up just like the *Sungari* did." He turned to Rona. "Can you transport us over?"

"At this distance we cannot. Of our teleportation the maximum range thirty-five thousand kilometers is."

Normally, Nog would have had to work through the problem, but to his amazement, a solution presented itself almost immediately. "Colonel, can you drop two EVA suits into

space and then move off?"

"I don't see why not. But I don't see why, either."

"Once you do that, Shipmaster Rona can move close to the suits and transport us into them. Then the Orelhoddish will move off and you can pick us up."

"A brilliant idea that is," Rona said approvingly.

"Preparing the EVA suits now," Kira said.

Ten minutes later, Nog and the unconscious Ezri were transported into the EVA suits. Five minutes after that, they were beamed aboard the *Defiant*.

Bashir was anxiously awaiting them in the transporter bay, and he immediately went to Dax with his medical tricorder.

Nog found himself with conflicting thoughts. He knew from Starfleet emergency medical training – his own, Jadzia's, and Ezri's – that you always checked the unconscious patient before the conscious one. But the part of him that was Lela – who was quite the ethicist – was cranky about him treating his own girlfriend, while the part of him that was Ezri was thrilled to see his beautiful face.

"YOU DON'T NEED TO DO ANYTHING EXCEPT REPORT TO THE MEDICAL BAY. IF I DON'T GET THE SYMBIONT BACK INTO EZRI SOON, SHE'LL DIE."

Kira was standing next to Transporter Chief Fnaxnor. Nog limped down off the platform – the EVA suit's left leg staying rigid for support – and looked at the colonel. "I need to modify the shields so we can approach the Orelhoddish safely."

Bashir stood up. "You don't need to do anything except report to the medical bay. If I don't get the symbiont back into Ezri soon, she'll die."

Nog had been afraid of that.

To Fnaxnor, Bashir said, "Beam her directly to the medical bay." Then to Nog: "Let's go."

As he followed Bashir out of the transporter bay, Nog said to Kira, "I'll have that shield modification for you once we're done."

Bashir had Nog sedated as soon as he got him out of the EVA suit. He

faded into unconsciousness, Julian's lovely face staring down at him.

And then nothing.

Both Kira and Bashir were standing over him when he woke up. The latter asked, "How are you feeling?"

"Empty," was the first word that came to mind. It had only been for a few minutes, but he had had gone from the memories of eleven people to just one, which was devastating. Bits and pieces of Dax's past hosts disappeared like wisps of smoke.

"You'll be happy to know that a new biosynthetic leg is being prepped on DS9. It should be ready by the time we get back. As for that empty feeling, with some help, you should be able to work on that –" Bashir them smiled. " – with our brilliant counselor."

Nog's heart raced. "Ezri's okay?"

Then Dax herself approached the

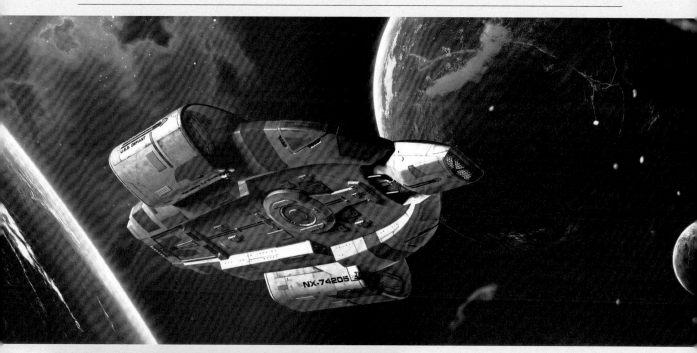

biobed, in a hospital coverall, pale from her injuries, but smiling brightly. "I'm fine, Nog. I'm Ezri Dax again."

Letting out a breath that he felt like he'd been holding since the *Sungari*'s systems started to fail, Nog said, "That's good."

Kira said, "When the doctor says you're ready, we can start your shield modulation plan."

And then Nog felt a completely different kind of emptiness. "I – I don't remember it!"

Dax put a comforting hand on Nog's shoulder. "It's okay – I *do*

remember it. At least, the theory – I've got no idea how to implement, but maybe I can talk you through it?"

They spent the next hour working together, Dax voicing all kinds of theories about shield nutation and Raejin Waves and so on that were at once completely familiar and totally new to Nog.

But they managed it. And then the *Defiant* was able to approach the Orelhoddish ship.

Once the modulation proved beneficial, Bashir, Dax, and Nog returned to DS9 in one of *Defiant*'s

shuttlecraft, as both still had significant recovery to do, leaving Kira to continue the first contact.

Sitting in one of the shuttle's passenger seats, Nog looked at Dax in the next seat over. The memories were gone, but the emotions associated with them hadn't faded. He'd *been* Dax, even if only for a short while, which meant he'd been Ezri. He felt like he knew her even better than ever, including the depth of her feelings for, and loyalty to, Bashir.

Nog no longer had a crush on Dax. He was now completely in love with her.

However, he was more determined than ever not to tell her.

Then she turned to look at him. She smiled, put a hand on his, and nodded.

Now Nog realized that she *knew* how he felt. After all, he'd hosted her symbiont, too.

And he was also sure that it was okay.

Returning her smile, he leaned back in the seat contentedly, her hand still on his. ⊥

Dedicated to the fond memory of Aron Eisenberg. We miss you, buddy.

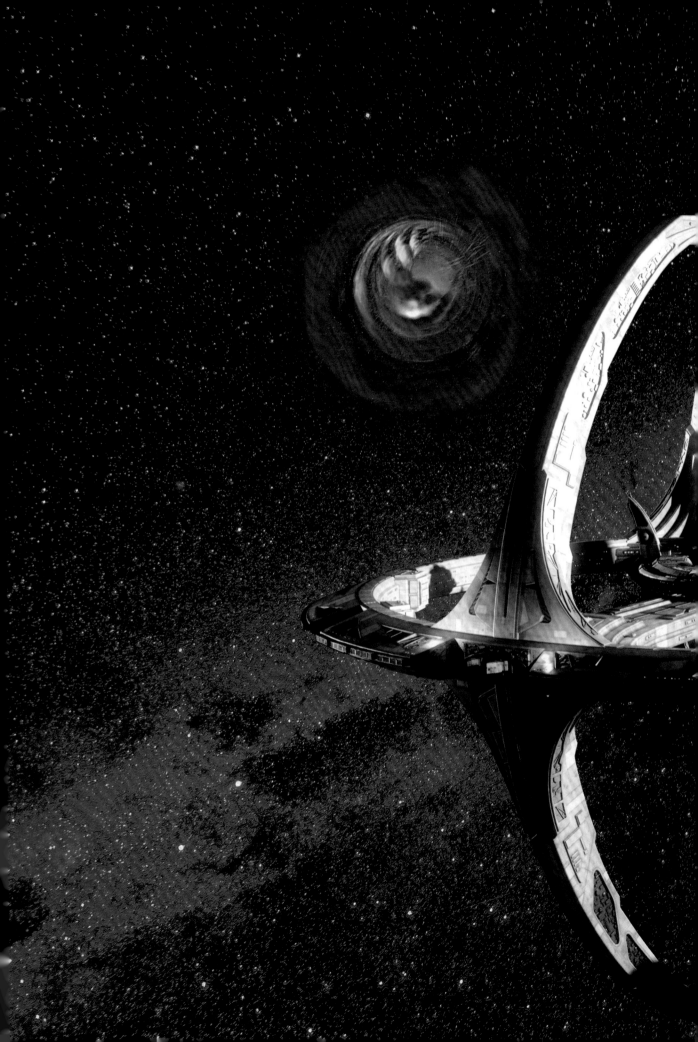

Summer Days Can Last Forever

STORY: MICHAEL COLLINS
ILLUSTRATION: MICHAEL COLLINS

ear Diary:

August 11th 1957

Sunday.

Finished *The Stars My Destination* and *The Naked Sun* that Mom got me from the library, Friday. Amazing!

I've re-read all my Supermans and Captain Marvels.

Missing Chet, Stevie and the guys, bet they're having just the best time at camp.

Mono *sucks*.

August 12th 1957

Nothing ever happens in Patterson's Creek. Another duuuuuuulll day.

August 12th 1957

Nothing ever happens in Patterson's Creek. Another duuuuuuulll day.

August 12th 1957

SOMETHING CRAZY HAPPENED!! Old Ned says he saw some kinda SPACE MONSTER LURKING BY HIS BARN!! Mom says he's 'in his cups' but I think he's maybe drunk again. Most exciting thing to happen in ages!

August 12th 1957

Nothing ever happens in Patterson's Creek. Another duuuuuuulll day.

August 12th 1957

Three strangers hanging around- a lady, an old guy and a youngish guy. They looked out of place. I waved but they wandered away.

The most exciting thing to happen in ages!

August 12th 1957

Weird – three strangers turned up and asked me about Patterson's Creek. The lady seemed kind but had that calmness some teachers've got?

I bet no one lies to *her*.

I told her I was Matty Redmond, that I was the only kid around as I had to miss camp on account of the Mono. She looked confused but the older guy? He said it was Gandhi? Glandu? fever or something.

The younger guy asked if I 'digged' Captain Proton? Like from the 30s?!! Was he older than my dad?!!!!

The lady said they had to go but they'd see me tomorrow. And they just vanished! Like Gully Foyle in *The Stars My Destination*!

I tried to tell Mom but she said I'd been reading too much Sci-Fi.

August 12th 1957

WEIRD – three strangers came up to me – they knew my name! A serious but nice lady, a grumpy old man and a younger guy. The old guy asked how my Mono was – I said I was ok now but then he wiggled a salt cellar at me as he held a cigarette case in his other hand. "Oh, I can sort this," he said.

The lady got testy with him like Mom does when Dad's about to do something he's not thought through.

"Are you sure that the right course of action, Doctor?" the old guy (Sure, like a 'Doctor' would wave condiments at you) shrugged and gave me what I guess he thought was a smile. "All better now."

The younger guy looked at his wrist as his watch beeped. "Captain- we're almost out of time." (a lady captain! Yeah, I could see it – I bet no one lies to her).

And then they vanished – like Gully Foyle!

I tried to tell Mom but she said I'd been reading too much Sci-Fi.

August 12th 1957
OK. This is freaky.
It's still Monday.
How can it still be Monday?!
And I feel great.
Like I've never been ill.
I went up to the lake, and those people just appeared out of thin air, like jaunting! Wild!

"Hi!"
The lady looked funny at me.
"You don't seem to be surprised to see us."

Guess I had the biggest, stupidest grin all over my face.

"You're the Captain! He's the Doctor! And-uh…"

The younger man smiled. "Tom Paris, Flight Control."

I punched the air.

"Yeah! You're spacemen! In disguise! I knew it!"

"Doctor – analysis? Previously no one was aware of the time loop, so luckily that scare when Knee-licks (Who?) accidentally breached the field got forgotten. How is young Matty here suddenly (she used a fancy word with 'cog' in it, but I figure she meant 'aware')."

Doctor waved his cigarette box at me.

"Curious. My procedure appears to have altered our young Mr. Redmond, so he is now aware of the time loop."

Tom got excited. "So curing his Glandular Fever did this? Could we

just do the same to everyone here? Give them Nanny-ites (I think he said this, must be a space word) and break the loop?"

They both looked at Lady Captain.

She thought hard about it.

"Not ideal, Mr. Paris. Instead of these poor souls repeating the same day in sweet ignorance we'd be consigning them to a living hell."

Doc shrugged. "Well, not for *long* –"

Lady Captain shot him a look that if her eyes had been a laser gun he'd just be pile of ash.

"I am quite aware of our accelerated time frame, Doctor."

Suddenly I was as scared as I've ever been.

"Say, what are you not telling me?! What's the skinny?"

"Matty, I am Captain Janeway. Kathryn. Yes, we're 'space people'. Though, actually, Tom and I were both born on Earth."

I looked at the Doc, was that what an alien looked like?!

Noticing, Captain Kathryn smiled. "Our Doctor is a… hologram – he-" She hunted for a word I'd get. "Um, he's like a …robot."

Doc looked annoyed "I most certainly am *no* –"

Captain Kathryn waved him quiet. She was so good at that.

"It's shorthand, Doctor. And as you yourself so delicately stated, we do not have the luxury of long explanations."

"Dr. Asimov wrote about holography, so I kinda get it?"

She looked at me again, like she was searching for a way to explain. I knew it must be real bad as she had 'that' voice, like when your Mom tells you your puppy got run over? But worse.

"Matty, do you know what day it is? What year?"

I told her – Monday, August 12th, 1957.

She nodded.

"To us it's a very, very long time after that I'm afraid. The year 2375."

I suddenly felt sick again, but not like with Mono.

"Captain –" Tom was pointing at his wristwatch "The aperture? –"

She put a hand on my shoulder.

"YOU'RE 'ROCKETS' REDMOND, BILL REDMOND'S SON? THE KID OBSESSED WITH SCI-FI, RIGHT? HOW'D YOU GET ON BASE?"

"We have to go. Be here tomorrow –" she smiled. "Well, today again, I guess… hopefully we'll have longer and we can explain more-"

And they vanished.

I spent the rest of the day trying to make sense of why three people from the future jaunted into our tiny burg? I knew I couldn't tell Mom and Dad- for one, they'd think I'd taken a crazy pill…

…and for another, they wouldn't remember it in the morning, would they?

August 12th 1957

This is *nuts*.

I *know* I wrote a long entry here yesterday but there's nothing.

And it's Monday again?

I had to go see Captain Kathryn and hope she had answers before she vanished again.

At the lake this time they were wearing overalls, not street clothes. Their Space Uniforms I guess?

Kinda disappointing.

They're not silver.

"Good Morning, Matty," she said, smiling.

"Hopefully, we'll have a bit longer here today – 7of9 (*was that the name of their computer? Cool!*) is working to extend the temporal aperture that allows us access to your town. I guess you have a lot of questions after yesterday."

Boy, did I.

"Why have you come back in time, or have we got rocketed into the future? And why do you have a Space Ship to visit Earth? And what was Doc talking about when he said we had little time?!"

She smiled, but it was a bit of a sad one.

"Where to start? We are the crew of the *U.S.S. Voyager,* and a few years back we got accidentally sent to a far distant corner of the sky –" She looked up, waved her hand somewhere towards the Eastern horizon "– that way, kind of…"

I was confused "Lost in space? So why are you here in the Midwest?"

Tom joined in.

"You ever think you're in… Nowheresville?"

Tom really was way older than he looked.

"Yeah… daddio." I smiled. He smiled back.

"Well, you literally are. Your whole town is on a planet a … gazillion miles from Earth. The only thing here. For some reason this day keeps repeating and we don't know why, or for how long. Unfortunately, you're orbiting a star due to go nova any time soon."

In my head I could see a big rock and on it, a bubble with our little town in it. With a big angry sun, ready to go bang. I knew what nova meant.

I'd read enough Sci-Fi.

I got real cold at that thought.

"But- how?! And how did you find us?"

Tom brightened – "That was me! I detected a transmission on a rarely used wavelength – the signal led us here!"

I said it could be something top secret from the army base the end of town?

"Um, no- It was an *I Love Lucy* rerun…"

"Army Base?" asked Captain Kathryn "That might be significant. Unfortunately, due to the time bubble, our scanners can't map your town, which is why we have to visit like this."

"Hey, a couple of nights back the base was all lit up, I guess something weird going on?" I said.

They seemed excited by this.

Captain Kathryn turned to Tom.

"That base might hold the key to getting Matty's people home-"

Tom suddenly looked excited – " – And us?"

"We'll have to see."

Captain Kathryn turned to me.

"Matty – going into an army base – we can only be here a short time, so we may need your help – this could be dangerous. It's asking a lot of you. Do you understand?"

I tried to be brave "Hey, if we fail, the day just starts again, doesn't it? And you said- someday soon this bubble's going to burst, right?"

Tom's watch beeped again,

breaking the silence.

Captain Kathryn turned quickly.

"Tomorrow – same time, meet us at the Base, we –"

They were gone.

I spent the rest of the day trying *not* to think I was living in a big soap bubble than could go pop any minute.

August 12th 1957

No entry again. I guess this keeps happening? But I guess I keep writing anyway?

I got to CAMP PERCIVAL as a jeep pulled up behind me.

"Hey junior –" I turned to see Tom, Doc, the Captain and a lady with Veronica Lake hair, all wearing military uniforms.

"You guys got dress up clothes for every day?" Tom smiled, Veronica Lake arched the eyebrow I could see.

"This is the child? Are we sure we need him?"

"We can only maintain our presence here for a few minutes, he's here all the time," said Captain Kathryn.

"Hop in!" called Tom. They covered me with a tarp.

Doc did all the talking. He was now a 5 Star General, had the right papers and was here to see the "artifact. No one questioned that he'd know. We drove to a remote hangar.

Tom got me out, after they cleared the site.

Inside the hanger was a (*crazy!*) little spaceship, barely three yards diameter. It was dented, shot at. But it glowed. Veronica Lake had one of those cigarette cases and waved it at the ship.

"Extraterrestrial in origin, a simple drone, probably an initial exploratory craft. They must have accidentally activated it. It is emitting some kind of time field. I can possibly reset it but –"

Tom's wristwatch bleeped "I thought you'd extended the aperture, Seven?"

She turned (wow, was she '7of9'?!)

"I did, Mr. Paris, however this field is interfering and we have no time to instruct the child how to –"

And then they vanished……
leaving me in this Super Secret Hangar as guards piled in, guns pointing.

The boss of the base, General Essex, had me in his office. He wasn't happy.

"You're 'Rockets' Redmond, Bill Redmond's son? The kid obsessed with Sci-Fi, right? How'd you get on Base?"

I told him, about the *Voyager*, and the Soap Bubble, and the day always repeating. It just made him angrier.

"Horse pucky! Why I oughta-"

"But General, you have a FLYING SAUCER –"

He held up his hand "That… vehicle we shot down, we've determined is a Russki spyplane. My scientists think they've worked out it's systems, got it all fired up- "

I exploded "But it's NOT! It's from SPACE! And we're <u>IN SPACE</u>! – and we're gonna –"

He grabbed me by the collar, dragged me out.

"Kid, get outta here – you're just kookoo, and a waste of my time –" At the gate, he said, "And if I see you again —"

"You'll never remember," I

NOTHING EVER HAPPENS IN PATTERSON'S CREEK. ANOTHER DUUUUUUULLL DAY.

muttered to myself.

August 12th 1957

Writing as I go. Dunno if I'll have a chance later.

I figured they'd try again, so waited by the gate.

They came. We got in (again). Straight to the Hangar this time.

7of9 talked me through equipment which was actually pretty straightforward.

Point and press.

"We have maybe five minutes til they come check," said Captain Kathryn. "You know what to do if we disappear again?"

I nodded.

While working, 7of9's hair fell away and I saw robot bits on her face.

I smiled.

She looked confused.

"Finally! *Real* Sci-Fi stuff!"

We didn't have five minutes. A couple of guards came early – Tom fired a laser gun at them, I was

shocked. He saw my look – "Hey, just stunned, don't worry." To the others, I said, "Maybe accelerate this?"

7of9 went through all kinds of super speed key tapping.

More guards entered, Captain Kathryn pulled me to cover, as Tom stunned those too. Doc strode towards the hangar gate and chewed out the approaching guards in a way that made General Essex look like a Milquetoast. It gave us extra minutes.

Seven looked at me. "They accidentally activated its homing system. As it could no longer fly its bubble took in the nearby area with it as it warped out. The resulting mass was flung across space, way off course. It keeps initializing its tachyon time-field, trying to relaunch, that's why the day repeats. I have fixed it and now it will leave as it intended. Your town will be snapped back in time and space, no

longer held in this self-regenerating matrix." She paused, looking at me. "In theory."

"What about you guys? Can you get home?"

She sadly shook her head "Not this time."

And vanished. They all did.

The guards Doc had been shouting at are stunned for a second, then notice me –

"Kid – Away from that! Don't make us shoot!"

But I can't – the sequence is almost complete, I'm tapping the last two pads to hit as I hear gunfire (firing high to scare me, I hope).

And –

August 13th 1957

Nothing ever happens in Patterson's Creek.

Another duuuuuuulll day.

Summer days can last forever… ✦

COMPLETE YOUR *STAR TREK* COLLECTION!

TV & MOVIE COLLECTOR'S EDITIONS

Star Trek:
The Illustrated Oral History:
The Original Cast

Star Trek Explorer Presents:
The Short Story Collection

Star Trek Explorer Presents:
'Q and False' and
Other Stories

Star Trek Explorer Presents:
'The Mission' and
Other Stories

Star Trek:
The Genesis Trilogy

Star Trek: Villains

Star Trek: Picard

Star Trek:
Fifty Years of *Star Trek*

Star Trek:
Epic Episodes

Star Trek:
All Good Things

Star Trek: The Movies

Star Trek Discovery:
Guide To Season 1 & 2

Star Trek: Voyager
25th Anniversary

AUTOBIOGRAPHIES & NOVELS

The Autobiography of
Mr. Spock

The Autobiography of
James T. Kirk

The Autobiography of
Kathryn Janeway

The Autobiography of
Jean-Luc Picard

Star Trek
Prometheus:
In the Heart of Chaos

Star Trek
Prometheus:
The Root of all Rage

Star Trek
Prometheus:
Fire With Fire

ART BOOKS

Star Trek: The Motion Picture
Inside The Art And Visual Effects

The Art Of *Star Trek:* Discovery

Star Trek: First Contact:
The Official Story of the Film

Star Trek: The Art of
Neville Page

Star Trek II: The Wrath of Khan
- The Making of the Classic Film

AVAILABLE IN ALL GOOD STORES AND ONLINE
TITAN-COMICS.COM | TITANBOOKS.COM

TITAN
MAGAZINE